EXPLOITS OF T[...]

*The Chalet School series by Elinor M. Brent-Dyer*

*Above is a complete list of Chalet School titles though only those set in bold type are available in Armada paperbacks. Unfortunately we cannot keep all these titles in print simultaneously but an up-to-date stocklist can be sent on request.*

ELINOR M. BRENT-DYER

# Exploits of the Chalet Girls

First published in the U.K. by
W. & R. Chambers Ltd, London and Edinburgh
This edition was first published in Armada in 1972 by
Fontana Paperbacks,
8 Grafton Street, London W1X 3LA

Armada is an imprint of Fontana Paperbacks,
a division of the Collins Publishing Group

This impression 1986

© W. & R. Chambers

Printed in Great Britain by
William Collins Sons & Co. Ltd, Glasgow

Dedicated to Muriel and Beryl Harrison and
Rosemary Jessup with much love

## CHAPTER I

# TERM BEGINS

IT was the beginning of a new term at the Chalet School, and all over the Chalet and its sister house, Le Petit Chalet, sounded a buzz of merry voices, a tapping of heels, and peals of gay laughter. Downstairs in the Staff Room, Mademoiselle Lepâttre, the Head of the School, was busy with such of her Staff as could be spared, discussing time-tables. Upstairs in the dormitories, Matron, with two mistresses, was overseeing the unpacking. In the Prefects' Room, the head-girl and all the prefects were exchanging holiday experiences in between doing a little work. For many of the prefects were new, and Jo Bettany, the head-girl, was supposed to get duty lists and responsibilities all arranged before the next morning. The first day was always more or less a go-as-you-please day. After that, the Chaletians settled down to ordinary work and play.

The eight girls who formed the prefect body at the Chalet School were all members of old standing. Joey Bettany, the sister of the co-Head Mrs Russell, Frieda Mensch, Simone Lecoutier, and Sophie Hamel had helped to make up the nucleus of the School when it was first founded nearly five years before. Marie von Eschenau, Bianca di Ferrara, Carla von Flügen, and Vanna di Ricci, the other four, had entered the school in its second term. They were all good friends, having gone up the school side by side, though Vanna di Ricci was rather older than the other seven. Joey was hail-fellow-well-met with most folk; her great friends were Frieda Mensch, Marie von Eschenau, and Simone Lecoutier. Together, they made a strong coterie, for Jo was a leader in the best sense of the word; Frieda possessed most of the common sense of the quartette; Simone was a clever, hard-working girl, whose chief weakness was a romantic affection for Jo which had survived nearly five years of teasing; and Marie, in addition to being Games prefect, was the school beauty.

Sophie, Bianca, and Carla were quiet, steady girls, who could be relied on to keep their heads and their tempers. Vanna had a motherly way which endeared her to all the small people at Le Petit Chalet, and she was the repository for half the secrets of the younger ones. So it will be seen that the Chalet School prefects were a strong body this year.

Jo was perched on the arm of a wicker chair, holding forth to Sophie and Bianca about the glories of the Guide camp which had been held in the summer holidays, and which she had attended.

"I think the hornets were the worst of it," she was proclaiming. "Lonny looked a *sight* with all the stings she got."

"No worse than you looked when Bill dragged you up out of that pit you fell in," said Frieda.

"Oh, well, it was all jolly, and I only hope we can have another next summer," was Jo's method of replying to this. Then she stood up, and looked round her. "Heigho! Another term! Anyone know anything about the new girls yet? I haven't seen them at all. Matey pounced on me to unpack as soon as I got here, and when that was over, I came straight here to see what you folk were doing."

"There are sixteen for here, and some for the Annexe, too," said Simone.

"Yes; tell us about the Annexe, Joey!" cried Carla von Flügen. "Have you seen it? And how do Juliet and Grizel get on?"

"You must see the Annexe for yourselves, my dears," said Jo. "As for Grizel and Julie, they'll get on very well, of course. Why not?"

"But it seems very funny that they should be teaching," laughed Simone. "Why, not so many years ago they were here, just girls, with us!"

"I think they will do very well," said Frieda quietly. "I know the children in their charge will be happy."

"I daresay," said Jo. "But what about the new girls, Simone? Seen any of them?"

"Only three—two sisters of twelve and ten, whose name is Linders; and an American girl named Elma Conroy. She is to be in the Third Form, I know, and I think Emmie Linders will be there, too."

"None for us, then?"

"Oh, no. And none for the Fifth, either. The Fourth have some; and the Second and the babies have most of the others."

A tap at the door broke into their conversation, and Frieda ran to open it. Standing there was their form mistress, Miss Annersley, the Senior English mistress, and a great favourite with the elder girls, though the Juniors stood somewhat in awe of her, for she had a sarcastic tongue, and was rumoured to be a great trial over preparation.

"Come in, Miss Annersley," cried Jo on seeing her. "How jolly of you to spare us a few minutes on first day!"

"I can't stay, thank you, girls," she said with a smile. "I only came to ask two of you—you, Joe, and Frieda—to come and see to the new girls.—Vanna, Mademoiselle Lachenais would like you to go over to Le Petit Chalet. They have six little ones over there, who are feeling very homesick and mothersick just now. Run along quickly, and cheer them up."

"Yes, Miss Annersley!" and Vanna jumped up from her chair, and went off to console six small people who had left their homes for the first time, and were feeling very miserable about it.

The Senior mistress gave the rest a smile, and vanished, saying, "I will try to come along for a chat later."

"I suppose we've got to go," grumbled Jo. "What a nuisance! I haven't done a thing about duties yet, and all my lists must be handed in to-night."

"Plenty of time later," called Marie von Eschenau after her. "See to the new people first, and when we have *Kaffee und Kuchen*, we can discuss duty lists in peace."

Jo nodded, and went off, followed by Frieda, to seek the new girls in the big form-room where they were congregated. The six First Form people were all over at Le Petit Chalet; but even so, there were ten here, all more or less bewildered by the buzz and clatter that went on round them; and one or two of them looking rather unhappy. Jo went up to them. "Welcome to the Chalet School," she said. "Hasn't anyone told you people where to go?"

"N-nein," replied a slim little girl of about twelve, with two long fair pigtails hanging down her back.

"Oh, can't you speak English?" asked Jo in German. "Well, never mind. You will soon learn here. Tell me

7

your name, won't you? By the way, this is Frieda Mensch who is Second prefect. I am Jo Bettany."

"Our head-girl," put in Frieda with a smile. "Tell us your names and which forms you are to be in, and then we can show you where to go."

"I am Alixe von Elsen," said the child who had spoken. "I am to be in the Fourth, I am told."

"So 'm I," said a jolly-looking girl of about the same age. "I'm Enid Sothern and I'm English, so I'm jolly glad we have to speak English here."

"Oh, you have to speak French and German as well," retorted Jo.

"Crumbs!" And Enid's face fell. "How ghastly!"

"Oh, you will soon learn," said Frieda comfortingly. "And many of our girls here will help you.—Shall I take these two to the Fourth, Jo?"

"Yes; do," said Jo. "Tell—let me see—tell Violet Allison and Ruth Wynyard to look after Enid; and Maria Marani and Cyrilla Maurús can see to Alixe."

Frieda nodded, and with an arm on the shoulders of each of the pair, steered them to the Fourth Form, where she called for the four girls Jo had named, and left the newcomers in their charge.

"Can't see why Jo didn't tell me," grumbled a bright-haired girl of about fourteen. "Guess I've been here longer than Greta and Vi."

"Yes; but they are more careful than you, Corney," replied Frieda.

Corney grunted, and turned back to continue her conversation which Frieda's entrance had interrupted, while the prefect went back to see what was happening to the other new lambs to the fold.

"Frieda, the Third get four news," cried Jo on seeing her. "And look who is here!"

As she spoke, she twisted round a ten-year-old child with short fair hair and a round rosy face, at sight of whom Frieda uttered an exclamation of surprise.

"Gretchen! I did not know you were coming."

"Der Grossvater said I must," replied the little Gretchen composedly. "Mamma cried very much, but Papa was pleased, for I shall see die Grosseltern so often, and that I cannot do when we are in Innsbruck. Also, I wished to come to the school he has spoken of to us."

"Good old Herr Braun!" cried Jo, naming the proprietor of the largest hotel in the Briesau Peninsula, the owner of the land and buildings of the Chalet School, and her very good friend. "Well, we're all glad to have you, Gretchen.—These," she went on to Frieda, "are Elma Conroy and Mary Shaw who are Americans. Elma comes from Virginia, and Mary from—*where* did you say, Mary?"

"Union, Mass.," replied Mary, a brown-haired, brown-eyed elf, with a demure air which, they were to find, was somewhat misleading.

"Lots of your compatriots here," said Jo cheerfully. "You won't feel lonely, I can assure you.—And this is Emmie Linders, also for the Third."

Emmie Linders was so fair, that her hair looked almost white. In startling contrast were her lashes and eyebrows, for they were black. A small child behind her was so like her, that Frieda guessed her to be a sister, and asked about it at once.

Emmie nodded importantly. "This is Joanna," she said in German. "She is just ten, and I am twelve. Die Mutter heard all about this school, so we are come, though there are good schools in Wien, too."

"Come from Vienna?" asked Jo. "We have another Viennese girl—Marie von Eschenau. I'll tell her, and she'll have a chat with you sometime."

"That will be the Herr Graf von Eschenau's daughter," said Emmie. "Die Mutter has met the Gräfin."

"Then you'll be all right," said Jo. She went to the door, and caught by the arm the bright-haired girl from the Fourth, just as that young person was rushing past. "Where are you going, Corney?"

"Just up to dormy," said Corney.

"Good! Go to the Prefects' Room on the way and ask Marie to come here, will you? Thanks very much."

Releasing her victim, Jo proceeded to introduce the remainder of the children to her friend. "These folk are for the Second.—Edelgarde von Rothaus, Linda Sonnenschein, Elsa Fischer and, of course, Emmie's sister. If you'll look after them, I'll take the Third Form people to their room, and give them over to Dorothy Brentham and Kitty Burnett."

Frieda nodded, and Jo went off after bidding Emmie wait for Marie's arrival. When she returned, she found the Games prefect chattering eagerly with the two little

Linders, while Frieda had vanished in the direction of the Second Form, whence she presently returned, and after warning Marie that it was nearly time for *Kaffee und Kuchen*, the two grandees strolled off to their own abode.

"Well, what are the new girls like?" asked Sophie Hamel as they entered.

"I think they look very nice," said Frieda thoughtfully. "Of course, they are only Middles and Juniors, so we shall not have much to do with them."

"I'm not so sure," said Jo slowly.

"Why, Joey! What do you mean?"

"I should say that English kid in the Fourth—what was her name—oh, Enid Sothern!—Well, I should say she's rather a handful."

"I thought her rather pleasant," persisted Frieda.

"Oh, she wasn't rude or anything like that. But she looks as full of mischief as a monkey, and the Fourth don't need any more of that kind."

"Elsie and Evvy and Lonny have all been moved up," someone reminded her.

"I know. But Corney is still in the Fourth. And Cyrilla and Maria will take their fair share in any monkey-tricks going. I should say Enid will add to the brightness of that form.—She looks like it, anyway!"

"What about the Third? Have they any mischievous genius?" asked Vanna, laughing.

"No; I don't think so. They have two Americans, though, one from the North and the other from the South. So Evvy and Corney and Louise have two more to keep them company."

"What about the rest?" asked Bianca.

"Oh, Firsts and Seconds are easily squashed. Besides, you'll have to ask Vanna about the babes. I know nothing about them.—Come in!" as a tap sounded at the door.

There was a wrench at the handle, and then two members of the Fifth Form—Margia Stevens, its head, and her great chum, Elsie Carr—literally tumbled into the room, wild with excitement.

"What on earth's the matter?" demanded Jo. "Can't you come into a room properly *yet*?"

They paid no heed to her scathing tones. They were too full of their own news for that. Giggling wildly, Margia announced, "Oh, Joey! We've got a new girl—just come—"

"She's sixteen," put in Elsie, determined not to be left out of it. "She has never been to school before—"

"Her father's something in the army—"

"And she thinks herself everybody on earth—"

"—And just—wait—till—you—see—her!" Margia wound up the duet in portentous tones, and the prefects looked at each other, wide-eyed.

"How d'you mean?" asked Jo at last.

"Her father—so far as we can gather—was a tremendous pot before the War," began Margia. "After it was over, they went away to live on his country estate, and she's been brought up like the books say they were—*you* know—officers are everybody, and everyone else the dust beneath their chariot wheels!"

"Do you mean like—"

"If you're going to say 'like Eustacia Benson when she first came,' not in the least," said Elsie. "*She* was only intellectual. *This* is a snob—an out and out *snob*! And we want to know what you think of it."

"I'll tell you later when I've seen her," said Jo cautiously.

CHAPTER II

EXPLANATIONS

FOUR and a half years before this story opens, Madge Bettany, accompanied by her young sister Jo and a French friend, Mademoiselle Lepâttre, had come out to the beautiful Austrian Tirol to try to found a school for girls on the shores of the loveliest of all the Tirolean lakes— the Tiernsee. The reason for this was that they had been left almost penniless, and Jo, always a delicate child, had been alarming them seriously.

The School began with eight girls, and speedily prospered. The girls were taught on English lines, though they naturally had to be tri-lingual, learning French, German, and English. The numbers began to mount, and when Miss Bettany married Dr James Russell, head of the big sanatorium on the Sonnalpe, at the opposite side of the lake, it was a most flourishing concern. Mrs Russell had never lost her interest in it, and was still regarded by the girls as their Head—"our dear Madame," as they called her. By degrees, the elder girls finished and left, some to go on with their education, others to go home, others still to marry. Of all these, two had come back this term as members of Staff. Up on the Sonnalpe it had been found advisable to open an Annexe to the school for delicate girls, and Grizel Cochrane and Juliet Carrick were there as Music and Head mistress respectively.

Of those who had married, Gisela Marani was the wife of Frieda Mensch's only brother, also a doctor, and lived on the Sonnalpe not far from the Russells. Marie von Eschenau's sister lived in Salzburg; and Frieda's sister, Bernhilda, was the wife of Marie's eldest brother, Kurt, and lived in Lyons. Others of the old girls were scattered about the Tirol, and all bore witness to the wonderful Chalet School, so that pupils were plentiful.

As for Jo, the years in the life-giving air of the mountains had completely driven away any further need for fear where she was concerned. She was now as wiry as a young mountain-goat, and, after working up steadily through the school, she was head-girl. It must be owned that there were many times when she wished it were not so. There had been almost a battle royal between the young lady and her sister before it had been settled. Jo had a dread of growing up, and she resented anything that reminded her of the fact that she could be a child no longer. Still, she was fairly reconciled to her fate now, and the girls often declared that she gave signs of being the best head-girl they had ever had.

After *Kaffee und Kuchen*, the prefects parted. Some of them were expected to go on duty with the lower forms, and others had work of their own to see to. Joey sat down in the Prefects' Room, and began to make out the "duties list" with much squirming and grimacing, and Simone Lecoutier had undertaken to copy out the school notices for the "General Notices" board.

Presently the French girl laid down her pen, and looked across the table at her friend. "Joey," she said.

"What?" said Jo crossly.

"I have news for you. It is really for all of us, but I wanted you to know the very first of all."

"Well; what is it?" Jo was getting into a bog over

prep duty, and was not inclined to be interested in anything else.

"I had a letter from Deira to-day."

"Oh?" The Head Girl laid down her pen too, and looked less bored. "What had Deira to say?"

"She tells me that she has been to France this summer, and she went to Lyons to see Bernhilda and Kurt. Here is the letter for you to read. You will be so glad to know that Kurt's firm has decided to move him to—"

"To where?" demanded Jo, even as she grabbed the letter.

"To Innsbruck," replied Simone. "Bernhilda will be near us all again. Are you not glad, my Jo?"

"Glad? I should just think so! How gorgeous to have Bernie and Kurt so near! I only wish there was some chance of seeing Deira. I suppose she says nothing about paying us a visit?"

Simone shook her head. "No; she does not speak of that.—Why do you stare so at me, my Jo?"

"Your hair! Simone Lecoutier, it—it's positively untidy! Why on earth don't you go and get it cut?"

Simone coloured furiously. "Because this year Maman has said that I must let it grow. I shall want to put it up when I am at the Sorbonne, and it must be long enough for that. It has not been cut since before our camp. I am glad," she went on thoughtfully. "Now I am growing up, I want to have long hair."

"Oh *hang* growing up!" retorted the Head Girl, as she unfolded Deira's letter. "That's all you folk ever think of these days! As for your hair, you'd better do *some*thing about it, or Matey will be on your track. You look worse than I do in my wildest moments."

As her own black mop looked more like a gollywog's wig than anything else at the moment, her remark was pointed. But Simone knew her Jo, so she only gave a little chuckle. "You had better let your own hair grow. Madame never has had hers cut."

"My sister's hair is curly, and mine's as straight as a barge-pole," said Jo. "Grow your own if you must; but leave mine alone. It's jolly comfortable as it is. I wouldn't have ends tickling my neck for anything—as *you'll* have if you go on!" She subsided into Deira's letter after this, and Simone picked up her pen and placidly went on with her copying.

Presently Jo laid the sheets down, and set her elbows on the table, leaning her chin on her clasped hands. "Deira's not much altered," she remarked.

Simone looked up. "Did you expect she would be?"

"I didn't know. She's been presented, and gone to balls and other stupid things. It *might* have made a change in her."

"Not in Deira," said Simone decidedly.

"May I have this letter to send to Grizel?"

"Yes; when the rest have seen it. But will Deira not have written to Grizel herself? They are great friends, are they not?"

Jo nodded. "Have been ever since—" She stopped suddenly.

"Ever since—" Simone prompted her softly.

"Ever since—*something* happened."

"But what do you mean, my Jo? Are you thinking of the snow-fight when Grizel was so nearly killed?"

"Well—I was," owned Jo, a funny look on her face as she recalled that fight. Something had happened then which Simone was not to know. The accident to which the French girl had referred had been no accident, but the result of a fit of temper on Deira's part, when she had picked up a stone in her blind fury, and flung it at Grizel. Only Grizel, Deira herself, Jo, and the school baby, the Robin (now at the Annexe), had known about it.

Simone saw the look on Jo's face, but put it down to the awful shock of Grizel's injury which had affected them all more or less badly at the time. She made haste to change the subject, and asked what was happening about duties.

"I wish I knew," said Jo.

"Why, how are they difficult?"

"Well, there are eight of us, and five nights for prep duty. I'm not very sure how to divide up—that's all."

"Why not leave that to the five senior prefects," suggested her friend. "That would be Frieda, Marie, Vanna, you and me. Then Sophie, Carla, and Bianca could share the Break duties between them."

"That's rather an idea," said Jo. "I believe I'll do that if everyone agrees. Break duty isn't bad—just to see that the babes get their cocoa and biscuits. It's over pretty quickly these days, when there aren't any lessons out-of-doors. Yes; if those three will agree to it, we'll settle that way. I wish they'd hurry up and come. I want to get this finished."

"They will not be very late," said Simone soothingly. "And what about the rest?"

"Oh, we'll discuss that at the meeting. What time is it? My watch has stopped, and I can't get it to go."

"It is seventeen and a half," said Simone. "Have you wound it up too tightly again?"

"I suppose so," said Jo gloomily. "Bang goes *more* pocket-money! And I had to send it to be mended twice last term, too."

"Well, suppose I go and tell the others that we will meet as soon as assembly is finished?" said Simone.

"Write out a notice and put it up—that's better than you running all over the school. I'd better get down to the library and see about the magazines. The bell will ring presently."

Simone set to work to write the notice, and Jo ran off to the room where the library was housed, and began turning over the piles of magazines which the School took in. This occupied her happily until eighteen o'clock when the bell rang for the assembly, and she had to hurry to the "splasheries" to make herself tidy.

When the whole School was assembled, it had quite an imposing appearance. At one end was the little dais on which Mademoiselle Lepâttre would take her place when she came. To the right of it were the basket chairs for the Staff, and the Sixth Form sat at the left. In front, were the rest of the girls, with the "babes" from Le Petit Chalet sitting on the floor, and the bigger girls graduating to the Fifth Form at the back. Most of them were there by the time the head-girl had reached her seat, though two or three people were hurrying over the last of their unpacking under Matron's eye. They came in two minutes later, and Matron herself followed them. Then the Staff appeared, one by one. Last of all, Mademoiselle entered, and everyone stood up. She went quietly to her place, and then stood smiling at them all, a plain-faced little Frenchwoman, but with something about her that spoke of her reliability and kindness. The girls would never think of her as they did of Mrs Russell, but they all had a warm feeling for her, and respected her deeply.

With a slight gesture, she waved them to their seats, and when all were settled, she spoke.

"Welcome to the Chalet School, all girls, whether new or old. I have not much to say to-night, and I know the prefects are anxious to get to their meeting. We welcome seventeen new girls to our midst, and I hope they will all be as happy as I know the rest of you are. This is the winter term, so I wish you all to take what advantage you can of the fine weather while it lasts. When the storms come, we may be imprisoned for days, as the old girls all know. Therefore, unless Matron gives permission, no one may be absent from walks or games. We hope to hold our annual sale of work next term, so the Hobbies Club will be busy. Guides, Folk Dancing, all our usual winter activities will continue.

"Now I wish to speak of our Annexe where, as you know, two of our own old girls are in charge. For the first week-ends, it has been arranged that you shall go up in sections to see it. You will go after *Mittagessen* on the Saturday, and stay till Sunday afternoon. As the new coach road is ready, we will go up in motor coaches, so that you may not be wearied by the long climb. Arrangements will be made for you to sleep at a small chalet Doctor Jem has had built near the Annexe for such a purpose. And for Half Term, it is hoped that all those who do not go home will be able to go."

She paused here, and Joey, catching various glances, jumped to her feet. "Thank you, Mademoiselle," she said. "It is awfully good of you all to take so much trouble, and we are very grateful to you."

Mademoiselle smiled. "It is no trouble, Joey. Also, I know that those who have little sisters at the Annexe will long to see them. But with regard to Half Term I wish to say that we expect all who generally go home to do so this time. Accommodation is limited, and we cannot take up more than our usual numbers. Now that is all. You may dismiss."

The girls rose, and quietly filed out, Mademoiselle Lachenais going off with her babies, while Miss Wilson and Miss Stewart hurried up to their own rooms to get ready for the walk with the Middles. Miss Annersley stayed to speak to Mademoiselle for a minute or two, and the prefects strolled up to their own room.

"It is a warm evening," said Frieda, looking out of the window at the late sunlight. "They say it will be a long autumn this year."

16

"Just as well when you remember what last winter was like," declared Jo. "It'll give the people a chance to get something saved."

The rest murmured agreement. They knew that when the winter was long, it frequently meant great hardship for the peasantry who live round the lake. Most of the people rely on the summer season when the hotels are open for their livelihood. Others of the men are cowherds while the cattle are up on the mountain alms for summer pasturage. But when the great beasts come down to the valley sheds for the winter, it means that work is less. The Tiernsee people are seldom far from starvation during the snowy months, and when a long winter comes, it may mean famine and sickness. The previous winter had been such an one. It had begun early, and continued until the beginning of March—nearly six months. The people had suffered, and the School was not able to help very greatly, though they had done their best. If this year's was to prove a long autumn, it would, as Jo said, balance things a little.

"We are to have Zita again," she said, referring to a great St Bernard which belonged to a family they knew very well. "Mercifully, her pups came in March this year, and they sold the lot. They'll have that money to live on, and two of the boys are in Innsbruck now, and send home money every week, so things are easier for them. My sister says that if we have Zita as usual, she thinks they will need no other help."

"There are any number who will though," said Marie.

"I know. We must discuss it later. At the moment, I want to get on with duties and school work generally. Got paper and pencil, everyone? Then we'd better begin. —Frieda, will you read the term's record, please?"

## CHAPTER III

## THE PREFECTS IN CONCLAVE

FRIEDA stood up; but before she could begin, there was a tap at the door, followed by the entrance of Mademoiselle Lepâttre.

"I am sorry to interrupt you, girls," she said, "but I wish to tell you about the new school arrangements."

New arrangements? This sounded interesting. Joey offered her own seat, and subsided into one pulled up to the table by Frieda. Mademoiselle sat down, and smiled at the expectant young faces turned to hers.

"As you know, girls," she began, "we have grown greatly this term. It was hoped that the new chalet would be ready to accommodate the Middles, but owing to various causes, it is still only half built, and I am afraid we shall not get it till next Easter. Also, so many girls—we are a hundred and five this term—has meant a re-arrangement of classes. There will be fourteen in the Sixth this year. The Fifth, we have been obliged to divide into two—Five A and Five B. This has meant that we had to engage at least one more mistress; and as the work will be increased, we have also engaged a junior mathematics mistress. In addition, we needed another form-room. Therefore, we have decided to take the Second Form over to Le Petit Chalet, to which three rooms have been added. They, with the First, will be there as Juniors always, and it will be necessary for you to arrange for their preparation as well as for the Middles over here. There are eight of you prefects, so that will mean that two must be on duty each evening. The remaining evening, the Staff will see to. The Juniors will be with you for games as before. Also, they will come over on the nights when the Hobbies Club meets. But I wish them to have their own library over there, so one prefect must act as assistant librarian so that she can attend to them."

"What about Break, Mademoiselle?" asked Jo when she stopped.

"The mistress last with them will attend to it," replied the Head.

"And morning walks?" queried Frieda.

"One of their own mistresses will be responsible for that also. Miss Leslie and Mademoiselle Lachenais are coming over here with Miss Wilson; and the two new mistresses, Miss Norman and Miss Edwards, will see to Le Petit Chalet. They have their own Matron there, too. Matron Gowland has enough to do over here. So at Le Petit Chalet the children will have Matron Lloyd." A little silence followed, and then she rose. "I thought it better you should know all this," she said as she prepared to leave the room. "It may help you in the arranging of duties."

Then she left them, and once she was gone, and Joey had resumed her own seat, a babble of tongues broke out that any bevy of monkeys might have envied.

"But what a strange thing!"

"The babes away by themselves—for that is what it comes to! Well, perhaps we shall have a little peace this term!"

"*Two* new mistresses? I wonder what they are like?"

"But did *you* know of this, my Jo?"

Jo turned to the last speaker—Simone. "Never heard a word about it," she declared. "It's as big a surprise to me as to you.—But as for peace, my dear Sophie, do you really expect that when the Middles are left us?"

Sophie, a big, pleasant-faced girl of sixteen, laughed. "Perhaps not. But at least we shall have more time to spend on the Middles."

"Then they will be twice as bad as usual," said Marie von Eschenau with conviction.

"Oh, come! Elsie and Lonny have been moved into Fifth, I know, for they both came screaming to me about it. That rather splits up the Quintette."

"So far as I can see," said Simone in her own language, "it simply means that there will be a triplet in the Fifth and a duet in the Fourth."

"I do not think that at all," said quiet Carla von Flügen. "I think it is likely that Elsie has been sent to Five A as she was top of the Fourth last term; and Lonny to Five B. Then Elsie and Margia will be together, and Lonny will be by herself, and Evvy and Corney will be together in the Fourth."

"If Lonny has been moved up," said Joe, "then Evvy has, for they were level last term. So *that* will leave Corney by herself. H'm! It looks rather as though our labours *were* to be lightened this year."

"Then let us set to work on the duties," suggested Frieda. "We have not much time, for *Abendessen* is early to-night."

Jo nodded, and Frieda rose once more, and read out the record for the previous term. It dealt with Guides—including the Guide camp of the summer holidays—games, the Half Term visit to Oberammergau when they had seen the famous Passion Play, and *The Chaletian*, the

School magazine. When it was finished, it was gravely "passed" by the girls, and Jo signed it as head-girl.

"Well, prep seems to solve itself easily," said the head-girl. "I suggest Frieda and Vanna for Monday; Simone and Sophie for Tuesday; myself and Eva for Wednesday; and Marie and Bianca for Thursday. One week we take Middles and the next Juniors. Is that agreeable to everyone?"

"Quite," said Marie. "But, Joey, Wednesday night is nearly always the worst night in the week. Is it fair that you and Eva should have it always?"

"Well, as head-girl, I ought to take it. But Eva needn't if she would prefer to change with someone," said Jo consideringly.

"Oh, but I do not mind at all," said Eva, a quiet girl, who generally agreed to whatever proposals were made.

"Then shall we consider that settled?"

They agreed, and Jo scribbled out the list accordingly.

"Now for the specials," she said when that was done. "Sophie will continue to be librarian, I suppose?—And you'll be Music prefect, Carla? You're the best, really. You know old Vater Bär, and don't drive him to the verge of lunacy by being too fussy; but you know where everything is as a rule, which is what the old growler wants."

In these rude terms she referred to old Herr Anserl, the visiting Music master who came up to the School from Spärtz, the little town at the foot of the mountain. He was a fine teacher, but possessed of a hair-trigger temper. Only the pick of the Chalet girls went to him for lessons, and Jo herself had nothing to do with him. She gave Miss Denny, the other piano teacher, quite enough to endure. As Margia Stevens had once said, there would have been no roof left on the school if Jo had learned with Herr Anserl. But in spite of all that, she and the gruff Music master were great friends, and Joey called him "Vater Bär" to his face, much to his own delight.

Now, Carla sighed, and agreed that she would still be music prefect; while Sophie beamed over the library.

"Hobbies comes next, I suppose," said the head-girl. "Frieda, do you feel inclined to take that on this term? I'll give you a hand, and so will Marie. We shan't get much in the way of organised games once the snow comes, you know."

Marie nodded at Frieda. "I will help all I can, Frieda."

"Well, then, I will do it," said Frieda, looking relieved at the thought that she would have help in what was often a most difficult task.

"Good! Simone, would you see to form-rooms and Staff Room? And you have my august permission to confiscate anything whatsoever you see lying about in either place—especially the Staff Room."

There was a general chuckle at this, for the Staff were, on the whole, a tidy crowd.

Jo chuckled too, then turned to Bianca.

"Bianca, could you cope with stationery, do you think? You know what it means—give out the things needed on Mondays, and insist on having a list signed by the form-mistress of each form. The ink monitress of each form will come to you on Friday afternoon for ink for her form. Anything else will probably come through the Staff."

"Yes; I could do that," said Bianca.

"Then I'll put you down for it," said Jo. "Eva, you'd better stick to pets again. You're very successful, and you know more about them than any of the rest of us do."

Eva laughed. "That is an exaggeration, Joey. But I will be responsible for them—all those I understand," she added cautiously.

They all laughed at that. In the beginning of the previous term, Cornelia Flower, always a firebrand, had turned up with a chameleon as a pet. Poor Eva, who was Pets prefect, had been sadly worried over this—more especially as Cornelia had calmly stated that she had no idea how it had to be fed or housed, and had looked to Eva for that information. Finally, the little fellow had been loosed in the garden where he had spent a glorious summer, catching flies by the dozen. During the holidays, when there had been one or two cold days, he had disappeared, and nothing further had been seen of him. Cornelia still hoped that he would turn up next year, but the others were not sorry that he had vanished.

"I don't think we've anything much beyond dogs and cats and rabbits this term," said Jo, answering Eva's remark. "Some of the babes have canaries with them, but their Housemistresses will see to those."

"And what is my duty, Jo?" asked Vanna di Ricci at this point.

"Well, not Break duty," replied Jo. "You did it all last term, and that's enough for anyone. Will you take on the Junior library? Mademoiselle said someone had to do it."

Vanna looked alarmed. "But I know so little about books," she protested.

"All the more reason to learn, then," said the head-girl austerely. "It's really just to see that the books are in good order and kept circulating. You must make a note of those which *don't* go, as it will mean we mustn't buy any more. And, of course, you must collect subscriptions."

"Oh," Vanna looked relieved. "I think I could do that."

"Good! Then I'll put you down for that. Well, I think that's everything so far as duties are concerned. Stacie will keep on the mag—and, by the way, they hope to get her down here by Half Term. She is making headway, and can sit up in her chair for quite a good time now. Jem says that when the cold weather comes, she will forge ahead, and she ought to be able to be with us by then. And, everyone, when she comes, I want us all to forget that dreadful first term of hers when she was such a little idiot, and take her as she is now—a jolly, decent soul! That accident has been the making of her."

"It has been a very hard making," said Frieda, with a thought for the girl whose entire spring and summer had been spent on her back, the result of an injury caused by her attempting to run away from the School when she had made herself so unhappy by her selfish, only-child ways, that she could endure it no longer.

"Yes. But it *has* done it. So we'll do as we did last term. I'll collect the stuff and sort it out; and then it can go to the Sonnalpe to her, and she can choose and arrange it. I'm going to put up a notice about it tomorrow, because I want everything in early. Then who-ever goes up that week-end can take it."

"Is that all, then?" asked Vanna.

"I think so. Anybody got anything else she wants discussed?"

"Yes. I should so like to know about this girl Evvy and Margia were discussing before *Kaffee und Kuchen*," said Simone plaintively.

"Oh, so should I!" Jo became animated at once. "Has anyone seen her?"

"I have," said Frieda unwillingly.

22

"What's she like?"

"Why not wait till you have seen her and form your own judgment? Besides, I've got news from Bernhilda for you all. Kurt's firm are establishing a branch in Innsbruck as an experiment, and they are sending him to take charge of it. So he and Bernie will be coming back next month, and will live in the Mariahilfe, on the next floor to ours."

"Bernie coming back!" cried Marie. "Oh, how wonderful! It did seem so dreadful when she went away to Lyons. But now, if she is at Innsbruck, and Wanda at Salzburg, and Gisela at the Sonnalpe, why, it will seem like old times. If only Mary and Rosalie and all the others could return—"

"Which reminds me, *I* have news for you," said Jo. "I'd forgotten about it till you mentioned Rosalie. She's coming out to the Sonnalpe as assistant secretary to the Sanatorium. Dr Jack shrieked it after me just as I left."

"Rosalie coming? How pleasant!" said Carla. "Juliet will be glad. She and Rosalie were good friends."

"She'll be gladder to hear about Bernie," said Jo with assurance.

"That is true, I think," replied Frieda softly. "She and Bernie were always so fond of one another."

"When does Rosalie come?" asked Bianca.

"After Christmas. She won't have finished her course till then."

"What a long time to wait! And Bette is to be married at Christmas, too."

"How d'you know?" asked Jo.

"Anita told me. She is very excited, for she and Giovanna are to be bridesmaids."

"And I, too, have news," remarked Bianca.

"Don't say that Luigia is betrothed?" exclaimed Jo.

Bianca smiled and shook her head. "No—not that— not as you mean it, my Joey. Luigia has decided, and last Monday she donned the novice's habit of a Poor Clare."

There was a little pause round the table. With the exception of Joey, all the girls were Catholics, and they knew what this meant. Jo, too, felt the solemnity of it. One cannot spend five years of one's life in a country where the Catholic Church is still the ruling factor and not learn something of it. Madge Russell was a broad-minded person, and Joey had attended almost as many Catholic services as Protestant. But this was the first of her friends to enter any Order, and she was correspondingly impressed.

"I hope she will be very blessed," said Frieda at last.

"She is very happy," said Bianca simply.

After that, the meeting turned to more mundane things, for they heard the sound of voices, and knew that the others were returning from their walk.

"Come along," said Joey, rising and stretching herself. "I simply must see this new girl. From all I can gather, she is the latest in freaks."

"She isn't a freak you will like," said Frieda shrewdly. "We have never had anyone like her in the School."

"We never had anyone like Stacie in the School till she came," retorted Jo. "*She* soon came into line. We must do what we can for this wonder!"

<br>

CHAPTER IV

## THE NEW GIRL

THE prefects strolled downstairs, laughing and chatting on the way, for rules were still in abeyance. As they came down, the side-door opened, and the Seniors came in, all looking very fresh and cool in their light frocks. September was hot this year, and the girls had all brought back summer dresses with them as well as the warmer clothes required to meet the rigours of the Tirolean winter.

They were led by Anne Seymour, a charming English girl, and her great friend, Louise Redfield, who came from America. After them were Arda van der Windt, Paula von Rothenfels, Thora Helgersen, and Luiga Meracini. These six, together with the eight prefects, made up the Sixth. The ten girls from Five A came next. After them, headed by Evadne Lannis, an obstreperous young person whose father, an American, was a millionaire merchant, and whose wife preferred the Tirol of her own birth, and Maria Marani, who possessed the distinction of being one of the first girls to come to the School and the younger sister of the first head-girl, came the Five B people.

This promising pair looked angry, as quick-eyed Jo noted when she met them. Evadne was scowling, and Maria was flushed. The rest of the Lower Fifth were no whit behind them. Something had upset even the placidity of Mercy Barbour, an English child of whom it was popularly reported that an earthquake would make no difference to her.

"Evvy and Maria," said Jo, "I want you."

The two followed her into the Sixth Form room.

"What do you want?" demanded Evadne truculently.

"To know what's happened on the walk. You don't all look as if you would like to slay the first person you met for nothing."

"It is that new girl—Thekla von Stift," said Maria. "She says that this is a school only for Burgher folk, and she will not stay to associate with the children of shop-keepers and the lower classes."

Joey sat down on the nearest desk. "She says—*what*?" she demanded.

"She calls us lower classes. Her father was an officer in the German Imperial army, and aide-de-camp to Prinz Oskar," said Maria, with a little nervous giggle. "She finds us beneath her in station, and she says she will write home and tell her parents that she cannot associate with such girls. They will take her away, she says, for they are as proud as she, and they belong to the Junker class—"

"Where *was* she brought up?" asked Jo in amazement. "Doesn't she know that all that silly nonsense goes for nothing nowadays? What is she—a Prussian?"

"Guess she's first cousin to Lucifer," said Evadne suddenly. "But if she is the Crown Princess herself, she shan't call Poppa names, and so I warn you! The little—"

"Now you be careful," warned Jo. "I know this is only first day, but you aren't going to come out with any ghastly remarks, even so. As for this Thekla von What's-her-name, you can just bring her along to the Common Room as fast as you like. I must inspect her."

With this, she got up as a signal that the interview was ended, and went off to join the others in the Common Room, while Evadne and Maria looked round for Thekla. She was standing by the window, looking disdainfully at the other girls. The whole of the Seniors used this cloak-room, and though a good many of them had gone to the Common Room, there were left Margia Stevens, head of Five A, Elsie Carr, her great friend, Cyrilla Maurús, a girl of four years' standing in the School, and themselves.

They marched up to the new girl, who stared at them, and Evadne took her arm. "Come on. You're wanted in the Common Room."

Thekla, a tall, fair girl of fifteen, stared at slim Evadne distastefully. "Will you please not touch me?" she said, withdrawing her arm from the young American's grasp.

"Afraid I'll give you typhoid?" asked Evadne with a grin. "You needn't worry. But Jo wants you in the Common Room."

"And who may 'Jo' be?" demanded Thekla haughtily. "Pray, why should I do as she wishes?"

"Jo is our head-girl," said Cyrilla, staring a little at such ignorance. "We always do as she wishes. It is the custom."

"Indeed! And *who* is she, this head-girl of yours?"

"She's Jo Bettany," said Elsie impatiently. "Her sister is one of our Heads, though she doesn't live down here, but up at the Sonnalpe. Jo has sent for you, and I'd advise you to hurry up."

Thekla looked at her; but she evidently decided to do as she was told, for she turned to the door. The trio followed at her heels, and were, as a consequence, close by when the new girl entered the Common Room, where the prefects were all assembled with the rest of the Sixth, and heard her speech as she came up to the head-girl.

"I am told that someone named Jo Bettany wishes to see me. I have come this once," was her ponderous an-nouncement.

For once, Joey was silent. She had sent for the new girl with some idea of welcoming her. As the only new Senior in the School, she must feel rather out of it, thought Jo. But this remark fairly robbed her of breath to say anything.

It was Simone, the ever-faithful, who replied. "This is Jo," she said, waving her hand in the head-girl's direction. "Jo, this is the new girl, Thekla von Stift."

Jo sat up and looked Thekla over. "I wanted to wel-come you to the School," she said. "I expect you know some of your own form by now, don't you?"

"They have spoken to me," said Thekla, "but we have not been properly presented, so I can scarcely have anything to say to them."

Once more the prefects were overwhelmed by the new girl; and once more it was left to Simone to reply for them. "One does not present schoolgirls," she remarked. "We make friends among ourselves."

"So?" said Thekla.

Marie von Eschenau came forward. "I hope—" she began.

But Thekla stared at her, and then interrupted her. "Why—it is Cousin Marie! What are you doing here, my cousin?" She spoke in German, and Marie promptly replied in the same language.

"I am here for my education. I had no idea it was you, Thekla. Why did Cousin Wolfram send you here?"

"I do not know," replied Thekla. "And you? How came Cousin Kurt to send you here? What can Friedel von Gluck think of such a school?"

"A little less of such talk, if you please," observed Joey, who had recovered her breath by this time. "This is a good school, a fine school, and we're all proud of it. As for Friedel, he has been here many times, and he thinks it an excellent school if you really wish to know."

Thekla looked disdainfully at her; but Marie broke in before she could say anything more. "Wanda finished here, Thekla. And I shall be here till next summer, I hope. Also Paula and Irma came. Irma is up at the Annexe just now, as she is not strong. But Paula was here a moment ago."

Thekla stared as if she could scarcely believe her senses. "But you consort with daughters of shopkeepers?" she exclaimed.

"Worse than that," said Jo drily. "Among the Juniors is one girl whose father was a sergeant in the British army, and whose mother was a lady's maid."

"But what can that matter?" asked Frieda Mensch in her soft, pretty voice. "Our Lady was the Wife of a carpenter. What difference can it make if we ourselves are good and kind and gentle?"

Thekla raised her eyebrows superciliously. "Perhaps *you* could scarcely be expected to understand," she said.

Frieda coloured, but Marie, who was very fond of her, flung an arm round her shoulders, crying, "That silly

27

Junker sort of talk won't do here, Thekla, and the sooner you realise it, the better! I am proud to have Frieda for my friend!"

"They have spoilt you," said Thekla. "My Cousin Kurt was always democrat in his views; but he might have had more thought for you, Cousin Marie."

"*Stop* calling me 'Cousin Marie' in that silly way!" cried Marie. "Use my name without any prefix, if you please. As for Papa, he thinks, as all sensible men do, that this is the finest school in the world!"

"A bit strong, that," said Joey with a grin. "Here— Elsie and Evvy—take Thekla away, and look after her generally, will you? Tell her what she wants to know." Then, as the two Fifth-formers went off with an indignant and puzzled Thekla in tow, she added to her own clan, "Those imps will soon teach her to see things in a different light."

"But, Marie, how comes it that Thekla is your cousin and that you did not know she was coming here?" asked Simone breathlessly.

Marie looked disgusted. "It's a distant relationship. My great-grandmother had twin sons. One of them grew up and married my grandmother, and the other married a Prussian girl named Thekla von Klavitz. We always knew that Papa's uncle had become very much Prussianised since his marriage; but we rarely saw them. I believe Thekla's father stayed with us when Kurt was a baby. But then the War came, and we saw nothing more of them. After the War, he retired to his estate in North Pomerania. He had been—"

"Equerry or something to one of the Kaiser's sons. I know that," said Jo.

"It was aide-de-camp," corrected Marie. "Well, the Government left him that estate and he married a second wife—his first one died during the War—and Thekla was born. I have heard Mamma say that his first wife was a very timid, gentle woman. She died when my cousin, Wolfram, was born. We don't know anything about Thekla's mother. And, of course, her father, who is also Wolfram, was a Prussian of the Prussians."

"I know," said Joey, getting up from her chair. "He was one of the people who thought that soldiers were everything, and civilians nothing. Evidently he has educated his daughter to his own ideas. Poor kid! I don't

28

envy her. She'll have a time of it before she comes down to earth."

"It will do her good," said Marie viciously. "She must learn consideration for the feelings of other people if she wishes to have her own respected." She glanced at Frieda as she spoke. Jo saw the glance, and tucked a hand into the arm of each of them.

"I think I'm sorry for this new kid. She seems to be a worse case than Stacie, and I thought *she* was the verge!"

"Oh, Stacie was suffering from swelled head on account of her scholastic attainments," laughed Anne Seymour. "She soon recovered from that. Listen! There's the bell for *Abendessen*! I can't say I'm sorry; I feel as if I could eat an ox."

"If that's the sort of appetite you've brought back with you," retorted Jo, "it's to be hoped they make you pay extra for food. Otherwise, I can see the rest of us going short on occasion."

They streamed out to the Speisesaal, where Thekla promptly became embroiled with Miss Wilson, who was in charge that night.

Miss Wilson was science and geography mistress in the School. She had been with them for four years now, and was regarded by the girls with great affection and not a little awe. She was tall, athletic, and had a pleasant face though she was not as pretty as one or two of the Staff. Never, since she had entered the School, had she been treated with anything but respect. Even Eustacia Benson, the "Stacie" of the girls' chatter, had not dared to argue with her.

But Thekla was a very different matter. She respected none who were not of the Junker class, and when the mistress gave her a seat between Anne Seymour, whose father, she had learned, was the proprietor of three big hotels in England, and Evadne Lannis, she demurred at once. "Your pardon, Fräulein, but I cannot associate with people like this," she said in her own language.

Miss Wilson stared at her, wondering if she had heard aright. "Why not?" she demanded.

"My father would not expect it," said Thekla.

Miss Wilson suddenly smiled. "Did he not send you here to school?" she asked.

"Yes; that is true," acknowledged Thekla, feeling rather uncomfortable at the smile.

"Do you think he does not know about our girls?"

"I scarcely think he can have grasped it. He would never have expected me to mix with girls whose parents are tradespeople and innkeepers."

Miss Wilson nodded. "He knows that we take girls of many classes here, and when he sent you, he agreed to your associating with them. That is all, Thekla. I am afraid you must sit where I have told you."

Thekla sat down, but with a very bad grace. She never opened her lips during the meal, though the rest were making the most of the first day's licence, and chattering as hard as they could in their own languages. It was understood that all girls must learn sooner or later to talk in English, French, and German; but there were Italians, Norwegians, Dutch, Hungarians and even one or two Polish girls, so the ensuing babel is indescribable. Miss Wilson was kept busy speaking any one of the three general languages as various questions and remarks were addressed to her.

Thekla watched the scene sullenly. She had come from an atmosphere which had nothing in common with this jolly school. Her father was one of the old-fashioned Junker class, who believed that the first men in the country were the army officers. All others were beneath contempt. The girl had been angry enough at being sent to any school. So far, she had had a governess who had been a weak-minded creature, bowing subserviently to her employers' orders. But this lady had unexpectedly married the pastor of the village near by, and Graf von Stift had found that it would be easier to send his only daughter to school for the remaining years of her girlhood than engage another. His wife had agreed. She was beginning to find her only child rather too much for her. Besides this, Wolfram, her husband's son, was coming home, and Wolfram had imbibed a great deal of the spirit of Young Germany, and she was anxious that Thekla should not be infected.

They had heard of this school among the Tirolean mountains through the parents of Eva von Heiling, who were acquaintances of theirs, and had entered the girl in the ordinary way. Frau von Heiling had assured them that it was a delightful school, and she had mentioned the fact that the little Crown Princess of Belsornia had been there for two terms. This had decided them. A Crown Princess, even of so small a state as Belsornia, *must* be "*hochgeborene*," and it was certain that the girls with whom she associated would be "*hochgeborene*," too.

So Thekla came, a Prussian to the backbone, to find at the very outset that she was expected to mix with girls of almost every class, and that her own cousin was specially friendly with Frieda Mensch, whose father was manager for a big engineering firm; while Maria Marani, to whose care she had been consigned, was the daughter of a cashier in a bank. Thekla was both furious and disgusted. When the meal was over, she had, perforce, to go back to the Common Room with the rest, but she refused to take any part in the dancing that followed, and was so curt to one or two girls who tried to befriend her, that they sheered off, and left her to herself.

Joey Bettany watched her between the intervals of dancing with all and sundry. "She's in for a bad time," she said to Frieda Mensch. "Stacie was bad enough; but she wasn't like that. I wonder if we shall make any impression on her?"

"Let us hope she will not have to run away and have an accident before she grows pleasant," replied Frieda, referring to the same girl. "Once of that kind of experience is quite enough. Shall we take yet one more turn, Jo?"

CHAPTER V

## THEKLA MAKES A SCENE

"PLEASE, Bianca, may I have blotting-paper for the whole form?"

Bianca di Ferrara looked suspiciously at Cornelia Flower and inquired, "But why, Cornelia? You all had it fresh at the beginning of the term."

"I know," said Cornelia, a sturdy girl of nearly fifteen, whose most outstanding features were a mop of bright yellow hair, a pair of enormous blue eyes, and a square chin. "You see, we've had an accident with the ink and had to use all our blotchy. Charlie was pretty mad about it, but she said I was to come and ask you for fresh."

"Have you brought a note?" demanded Bianca.

"No; Charlie hadn't time to write it. She said I was to ask you, and she would give you the note herself later on."

Bianca considered. The Fourth had the reputation of being the naughtiest Form in the School. Still, she did not see how they could get into mischief with blotting-paper.

"Very well; I will give it to you," she said finally. "But if I do not get the note, you will receive no more till after the Half Term."

"Guess you'll get it all right—unless Charlie forgets," said Cornelia. "You'd better ask for it if she does."

Bianca turned to the stationery cupboard and took out the blotting-paper. "How many pieces?" she asked.

"Eighteen, please," said Cornelia.

The blotting-paper was carefully counted, and with it in her hand the head of the Fourth was presently racing down the passage. The prefect put back the rest, and prepared to lock the cupboard. But just then, Thekla von Stift appeared.

"Do you want anything?" asked Bianca, somewhat impatiently, for the stationery monitresses had been rather dilatory that day, and she had been at the cupboard much longer than usual.

"An exercise book," said Thekla shortly.

Bianca stared. As a new girl, Thekla had begun the term with an entire range of new books, and it seemed impossible that she could need any more after just a fortnight.

"Which subject?" she asked.

"How should I know?" said Thekla impatiently. "I would become a new exercise book."

Bianca felt inclined to giggle at this literal translation of the German idiom; but Thekla had not spent a fortnight in the School without them finding out that she was painfully touchy and given to flying into rages at the smallest provocation. The prefect fastened on the important point. "But I must know which subject it is, for otherwise I do not know which colour to give you," she said.

"What does it matter? I am no child to cry because I have a purple book for my French exercises instead of a green one. Pray give me the book and let me go."

Bianca shook her head. "I may not do that. You must tell me which colour you wish. I must keep close account of all I distribute," she said.

Thekla looked black. "I have told you. Give me—give me a blue book," she said.

"Blue? Then it is for German *Dictat* that you want it? Have you the note from Mademoiselle Lachenais?" inquired Bianca, holding out her hand for it.

"No; I have not."

"Then I fear I may not give it without."

Thekla frowned, and stamped her foot. "But I say that I need it. What should I know of your rules? Do you fear that it will not be paid?" she asked.

"No; of course not," said Bianca, beginning to lose her own temper. "But rules must be kept. I cannot give so much as one pencil without a note from a mistress."

For reply, Thekla deliberately went into a rage.

"But I will have it!" she screamed, flinging herself at the cupboard, and snatching at a pile of exercise books which stood at the edge of the shelf.

As it was still near the beginning of term, the cupboard was full, and the natural result of this was to send the books to the floor. Some pencils followed them, and an opened box of pen-nibs. Bianca made a leap to try to save them, and contrived to swing the partly-opened half-door on to the Prussian girl's shoulder. The lock caught her blouse sleeve and tore it, and also scratched her arm slightly. Bianca exclaimed aloud at this, but Thekla gave her no chance to do more. Standing in the corridor, clutching at her arm, she uttered another scream, and then began to shriek her woes for all to hear.

"Ach, es ist schrecklich! Du bist eine Affe! I will become a book, and then you the door of the cupboard on me throw! Ach—*ach*—ACH!"

Her screams quickly brought a small crowd to the scene, though most of the girls were out in the playing-field and were hard at tennis and hockey. But Joey from the Prefects' Room, where she had been groaning over some returned geometry; Marie from a music-room; Mademoiselle Lachenais from her own form-room; Miss Annersley from the Staff Room, and Matron from the linen cupboard—they all hurried to the spot, to see Bianca standing looking horrified, while Thekla was stamping and raving up and down the corridor.

Matron took charge promptly. She had been three years at the School and had dealt with girls of all kinds most effectively. It was scarcely likely that she would be troubled by an hysterical Prussian. Taking Thekla by the shoulder, she gave her a little shake to remind her of where she was, and demanded to know the cause of all the trouble.

"It is this Schweinhund will not give me the book I ask, though she has just sent one girl away with a pile of blotting-paper!" shrilled Thekla.

"That's quite enough," said Matron severely. "You may not use such language here, whatever they may have allowed you to do at home. And as for screaming just because you can't get what you want, I never heard of anything so childish in my life. You must have taken leave of your senses—"

Matron had good reason for thinking this next moment, for Thekla deliberately spat in Bianca's direction, and then flung herself on the floor.

Miss Annersley bent forward, and dragged her to her feet, while little Mademoiselle Lachenais paled with horror, and uttered little staccato exclamations.

It was left to Joey to finish things.

"What a disgusting little object," she said in German in which they had all been speaking. "I never saw such disgraceful manners anywhere!"

Thekla spluttered with indignation, but was too furious to speak coherently. Miss Annersley took advantage of her state to remove her, asking Matron to come, too. Matron went after them, and Bianca, still rather white, quietly shut and locked the door after she and Marie had gathered up the spilt things. Marie looked especially glum, and Jo understood.

"It's not your fault, Marie," she said. "No one blames you for this. But how on earth has she been brought up?"

"I told you that Cousin Wolfram was a Prussian of the Prussians," wailed Marie, who was nearly in tears. "I suppose they have let her have her way. But what terrible behaviour! Surely she will not be allowed to remain, Jo? And if she is sent away, that is fresh disgrace to us, for she *is* my cousin, even though I do not like her in the least."

Jo looked thoughtful. "I doubt if she'll be sent away for bad manners," she said. "There'll be a fuss, of course.

34

Mademoiselle won't allow that sort of behaviour.—What really happened, Bianca?"

Bianca gave them an account of the scene between herself and Thekla.

Jo nodded. "I see. I expect she thought she could have things for the asking. She *is* the limit, isn't she?"

"Pauvre petite," said Mademoiselle Lachenais suddenly. "She must remain here and learn to control herself. I will go to her now."

She sped off, and the three prefects were left looking at each other.

"I must return the key to the Staff Room," said Bianca at length. "What do you do, Jo?"

"Go out to games, I think," said Jo. "I can't settle down to Geom. after a doing of that kind."

"And I will finish my practice later," added Marie.

"Then we will meet at the door, shall we?"

"Yes," said Jo. She stopped, and fidgeted for a moment. Then she suddenly said, "I say, you two, I don't think we'd better say anything about all this to the others. Let's give her a chance. She may feel better now she's blown up. We might try, anyhow."

"I agree," said Bianca, who was a peaceable person and hated trouble.

"I am glad of that." Marie's face lightened as she spoke. "I should not like the Juniors to hear of it at all. And Paula would dislike it, too."

"Shall you tell Paula?" asked Jo curiously.

"No; I think not. There is nothing to be gained by it; and, as you say, Jo, she may be better now."

So when the three prefects met the others, they said nothing of what had occurred, and none of the other girls ever knew anything about it.

The Staff, however, were told all that there was to be told. Matron applied a cold sponge to Thekla before she succeeded in bringing her to her senses, and then Miss Annersley insisted on knowing what had caused this. When she had been told, she scolded the girl soundly. But after that, she sent for Simone Lecoutier, and bade her take Thekla to the tennis courts and give her a good set of tennis. Thekla went because the mistress's manner overawed her in spite of herself. Simone called Eva von Heiling and Anne Seymour to oppose them, and Thekla forgot her troubles for a little in the match that followed.

Meanwhile, Miss Annersley, who was Acting-Head in the absence of Mademoiselle Lepâttre—the latter was up at the Sonnalpe for a few days to discuss business with Madge Russell—called a Staff meeting, and laid the case before them.

"We can't do much but keep an eye on her," said Miss Wilson. "She's a tiresome kind of child. And, of course, she'll have to give up these silly notions of hers of being one of the chosen people."

"The girls will put an end to that," said Miss Stewart—known throughout the School as "Charlie." "She's in Five B, and they won't stand any nonsense there."

Miss Leslie, who taught mathematics, and was form-mistress to Five B into the bargain, laughed. "They certainly will not. But do you think it advisable to let them treat her to the same teasing as they would mete out to other girls? If to-day is anything to go by, it seems likely that we shall have trouble in that case."

"Oh, we can't make exceptions," said Miss Wilson briskly. "Look at Eustacia Benson. We never worried about her, and what a nice child she is turning!"

"Eustacia was rather a different story. It's true she boxed Kitty Burnett's ears; but she would never have lowered her dignity to make such a scene as Thekla seems to have made," said Miss Annersley.

"But, Nan!" protested Miss Wilson.

"Oh, I know. I don't mean that we should watch the children. Only, I don't think we want any more of such scenes."

"Then what do you propose to do?"

"Give them all so much to do, that they have no time for teasing," said little Miss Nalder, the Games mistress. "We never know when the snow will come and put a stop to the games. I vote we see that they have games and walks and so on out of lesson time, until they are so tired they are thankful to sit down and rest when they do get home. Then, by the time the snow comes, Thekla will have settled down, and we shall have a little peace. What do you think?"

"Well, we can try it," said Miss Annersley doubtfully. "When do you want to begin?"

"To-morrow. They have Guides in the morning. I suggest we should have *Mittagessen* immediately after Guides, and then all get ready and go for a long tramp some-where."

"Well—where?"

"Why not up past Lauterbach, and beyond to the Mondscheinspitze?" suggested Miss Wilson.

"Better still; take them up the Bärenbad Alpe, and let them have *Kaffee* there. Then we can climb along to that queer little village you came through last winter when the path broke away near the Dripping Rock," said Miss Stewart. "You *can* get to it that way, can't you?"

"Yes; Nan and I did it in the spring," said Miss Wilson. She laughed. "Shall we ask St Scholastika's to come with us?"

"No, thank you!" cried Miss Nalder. "We shall have enough to do with our own little ones."

"Oh, I don't think the babies can come," began Miss Annersley.

"Oh, but can't they go to the Bärenbad Alpe for *Kaffee*?" coaxed Miss Stewart. "Their own Staff can bring them down after that, while ours go on with us. How many will go with the girls?"

"I will, for one," said Miss Wilson. "Nan, will you come?—And you, Kath?"

Miss Leslie nodded. "Rather! I've never been that way before. Let us hope the outing will help to bring Thekla to her senses."

"What about the girls who go to the Sonnalpe?" asked Miss Wilson.

"That is all right," replied Miss Annersley. "Dr Jem is coming down for them in his car. Only Joey, Simone, Cyrilla, and little Peggy Burnett are going. He will be here in time for *Mittagessen*, and we can leave them to him quite safely."

"Then we will consider it all settled," said Miss Nalder. "Well, I must go now."

The rest of the Staff were also due elsewhere, so they parted, and all the School heard of it was that they were to have one of the expeditions in which their souls de-lighted. Joey raised an outcry that the chosen day should be one on which she was absent; but Simone merely shrugged her shoulders, and vowed that a little peace would be grateful.

## CHAPTER VI

## UP THE BÄRENBAD ALPE

SATURDAY dawned clear and bright. Thekla rose with a feeling of sulkiness which drew a scowl between her brows, and dropped the corners of her lips. The rest were in high spirits. The Yellow dormitory nearly got itself excluded from the walk, for they indulged in pillow-fighting, to the detriment of one electric bulb and two pillows. However, Matron proved to be in a lenient mood for once, so she stopped short at scolding them all round.

Guides went with a swing as usual. Thekla had refused to join, since it was an English institution, and she never let slip an opportunity of showing her contempt for the English and English customs. She had to go for needlework to Matron, who resented this using of her precious time, and who had been heard to wish that Guides could be made compulsory. There were very few girls in the School who did not belong to either the Cadets, Guides, or Brownies. Thekla was the only girl of her own age to stand out. She needed little overseeing, it is true, for her sewing was as beautiful as that of most Continental girls is. But Matron always felt that the fewer girls she had to supervise the better.

Dr Jem appeared at the *Mittagessen*. He was a tall, fair man, with a keen, clever face, blue eyes that twinkled, and the long, slender hands of a surgeon. He and Joey were always great friends, and the girls were all very fond of him, even though he had carried off their beloved "Madame," settling her at the Sonnalpe, whence it was frequently impossible for her to come once the winter snows had fallen.

After the meal was over, all girls going on the expedition hurried off to change into their usual scrambling kit. This consisted of short skirts of rough brown tweed, with white jumpers, strong climbing-boots, and brown berets to match the skirts. They carried raincoats rolled up on their backs, and wore gauntlet gloves. The four people who were going up to the Sonnalpe merely donned coats and caps, and went off in the car with the doctor, carrying their cases with them, for they were to stay up until early on Monday morning, when someone would bring them down.

Thekla looked askance at her short skirt, but the rest wore them, so she submitted, and was quickly ready. Joey's last words to Marie and Frieda had been an injunction to keep an eye on her, and stop the Fifth from teasing her.

"We don't want any fusses," she remarked. "Just remember what's been the consequence of a fuss up the Stubai, and avoid anything further."

The two prefects promised her that they would do their best.

"Not that we can *always* watch the Fifth," said Marie rather dolefully.

"P'raps not," said Jo. "But you *can* watch Thekla."

Accordingly, when partners were being arranged, Marie went across to her very unpleasant cousin, and suggested that they two should pair off as "croc-in" was necessary.

They set off as soon as they were all ready. The "Babies" went with their own mistresses, for it was scarcely to be expected that they could keep pace with the elder girls. The Sixth Form led with the two Fifth Forms, Miss Annersley and Miss Stewart with them. Then came the Fourth and Third in charge of Miss Wilson, Miss Leslie, and Miss Nalder.

The way led across the playing-field, and out of a wicket-gate at the bottom; then through a kind of wild meadow-land, where heartsease still lifted their pretty heads, and occasional bushes of alpenroses were to be seen.

"The flowers are nearly over," remarked Marie to Thekla. "You should have been here in the summer. All this was one mass of wild flowers."

"They are very beautiful," said Thekla stiffly. "At the same time, I prefer to see flowers in a garden, where they are neatly tended. Wild flowers look so untidy."

"Perhaps they do," said Marie, struggling bravely to make conversation. "But don't you think they are just as lovely in their own way?"

"All nature has a certain beauty," replied her cousin primly.

"And it is so very lovely here," said the prefect; "even

in winter, when the snow is on the ground, and it is what Joey calls 'Christmas Card Land.' The trunks of the pines look so black against the white snow; and when it is night, and the stars and the moon shine down on it, and every frost-crystal glimmers and sparkles, it is wonderful."

"It must be," said Thekla, and let the subject drop.

"Have you been in the mountains before, Thekla?" asked Marie when the pause threatened to become too long.

"We have been in Switzerland, but I did not like it. There are so many tourists there, and they make such foolish remarks. I find that the English are so incapable of appreciating the beauties of nature."

Marie opened her lips to repudiate this remark; then she closed them again firmly. It was no part of her policy to quarrel with her cousin. So she led the way in silence to a rough road, flanked on one side by the rocks of the mountain, and on the other by a stout railing of tree-trunks.

"We go up here," she said.

At this point, the girls might break ranks and walk as they chose, so long as they did not get either too far ahead or loiter. Frieda Mensch, with Vanna di Ricci and Sophie Hamel, dropped back to join Marie and her un-amiable partner; and Frieda, with some idea of helping matters, began to chat pleasantly about the district. She knew it very thoroughly, for her father had been born there, and many holidays had been spent there by the family. The other girls joined in; but Thekla walked straight ahead, never seeming to pay the smallest attention to the conversation.

Thinking that perhaps she felt shy about talking with the prefects, Frieda presently spoke to the new girl directly. "Do you know our land at all, Thekla?"

Thekla said nothing. Marie nudged her. "Didn't you hear, Thekla? Frieda spoke to you."

"I heard," replied Thekla frostily. "No; I do not know this land at all. It is, doubtless, very beautiful; but I prefer the Fatherland."

"That is natural, I suppose," said Frieda, who was peacemaker to the School at large. "But don't you like Tirol, now you are here?"

"I cannot say that I am enthralled by it."

Even Frieda the peaceful nearly gave it up after this.

As she said later, "It's so difficult to go on talking when you're snubbed every time you open your lips."

However, Sophie Hamel took a hand at this point. "Ah, you have seen so little of it yet," she said cheerily. "We have not been back at school very long, and this is our first real expedition. We must wait for the summer, when we often go to other parts. Then you will see how lovely it is."

Now Sophie was, according to Thekla's views, even lower in the social scale than Frieda, for her father owned a big drapery business in Innsbruck. How Thekla had found this out was never known. It is quite probable that Sophie herself had said something, for she was very proud of the business, which had been begun in a tiny establishment in a little side street, and had grown till now it was the huge building in the Mariatheresien Strasse, the chief street in the city. But Thekla recked nothing of this. Her absurd training had taught her that trades-people were not fit to associate with those who, like herself, were *hochgeborene* ("well-born"). She therefore considered it a great piece of impertinence on the part of the elder girl to address her, and said so. "Will you kindly address yourself to your equals and not to your superiors?" she said insolently.

Sophie turned red, and her eyes darkened ominously. Marie flushed, too.

Luckily, Frieda still kept her head. "As Sophie is a prefect, and you are only in Five B," she said quietly, "I think you are making a big mistake in speaking as rudely as you have done. But as you are new, and perhaps don't understand about the prefect system, she may forgive you."

Sophie mumbled something; but she was wildly indignant in her heart, and it would be long before she forgave Thekla for what she had said. Frieda, seeing this, glanced at Marie, and that young lady rose to the occasion at once.

"Come, Sophie!" Marie exclaimed. "Let us run on and join Carla and Anne. I want to talk to them about library, and we may as well use this opportunity." She took Sophie's arm, and hauled her off, and Thekla was left with Vanna and Frieda who looked at each other.

Both wanted to set this very unpleasant new girl right; and both were rather shy about doing it. But Frieda, though she was quiet, and "very backward about coming forward," as Joey had once phrased it, was also very conscientious. She felt that she ought to say something to this haughty girl and set her right before her own form took a hand in the reformation. Better that she and Vanna should do it if possible. "May I say something to you, Thekla?" she asked in her soft, pretty voice.

"Speech is free," said Thekla coldly.

"I know. But you may not like what I wish to say. Only, I think that if I do not, someone in your form may; and, perhaps, not so nicely."

Thekla looked at her scornfully. "Do you think I care for anything those girls may say—those girls, many of whom come from the trading classes?"

"Yes; *that* is it," said Frieda, seizing on this opening. "It is this, Thekla. We never trouble about what our fathers are. The thing we think of is what we ourselves are. It is true that many of our girls come from the trading classes—"

"Yes; and I cannot think why girls like yourselves, whose fathers are in professions, would be friendly with them!" burst in Thekla. "There is as much difference between them and you as between you and us."

Vanna began to laugh. "Do you always write *Us* with a capital letter?" she asked.

Thekla flushed angrily. "I do not understand why you should laugh. There are classes the world over—"

"Ah, but that sort of nonsense is quite finished," said Frieda. "When such terrible things have been happening—"

"Look at Russia," put in Vanna. "They've turned out the nobility there."

"And those who are *hochgeborene* have to work at sweeping crossings and washing floors," said Frieda impressively. "And we are only schoolgirls. What can that sort of thing matter to us? Be advised by us, Thekla. Drop all these foolish ideas, and become one of us."

"And if I do not?" asked Thekla with as much insolence as she could compass in her voice.

"Then I am afraid you will be one on your own," said Vanna. "Frieda, Miss Annersley is calling you."

"I didn't hear her," said Frieda, as she set off up the rocky path to find out what the Senior mistress wanted.

42

"And—if I prefer to be alone?" asked Thekla of Vanna in choking tones.

Vanna looked at her. "Oh, well, if you feel like that—" she said, and left her sentence unfinished, for at that moment there arose from the slopes below them such a yelling as sent her tearing back to find out what was wrong. Thekla followed her, not knowing what else to do.

Now the path up the Bärenbad is bordered on the outer side by shrubs and bushes. In the season, wild strawberries grow thickly here, and the girls often gathered baskets of them. As September had come and was almost gone, the strawberries were a thing of the past. But blackberries were growing just as profusely, and it had dawned on some of the Middles that they would be just as nice as their sisters of the summer.

No one had any objection to their gathering some so long as they only attacked the bushes at hand. But Cornelia Flower, Enid Sothern, Klara Melnarti, and Jeanne le Cadoulec were not satisfied with this. In any case, the children from the valley had pretty well stripped the bushes, and what were left were very poor or else out of reach altogether.

"I just despise these," said Cornelia to Enid, in whom she had found a friend after her own heart. "Guess I'll see what I can get at the other side."

"Won't there be a row?" asked Enid.

"Let there," retorted Cornelia, with disgraceful grammar. "Come on—unless you're a 'fraid-cat!"

That was all that was needed. "I'm no more afraid than you! *I'm* not a funk!" returned Enid hotly. "But how can we get at them?"

"Where's Bill and the rest?" asked Cornelia.

"Bill's on ahead with Greta and Vi," replied Enid, after looking round. "Bonny's busy pinning up Kitty Burnett; and Nally's back there with some more of the kids."

"Come on then—an' mind where you're going!" And, with no more ado, Cornelia wriggled through the fencing, and made for a bush at some little distance, on which gleamed the purple-blue of great ripe blackberries.

Enid followed her example, and Jeanne and Klara, who had been just behind them, saw what was happening, and followed suit.

Later on, someone asked the intrepid four why they

thought the village children had neglected such a bush. They were accustomed to scrambling about the mountainside from their babyhood, and the bramble trails were not so very far from the path. Cornelia replied that she had given no thought at all to the matter. She had just seen the fruit and gone for it.

What no one had bargained for was to find that there was a sudden crack in the earth, and the small American, leading the rest, and not troubling to look where she was going, discovered it in the simplest way of all—by plunging feet first into it. The horror felt by her companions in evil when she vanished as if the earth had swallowed her up, may be better imagined than described. Klara and Jeanne promptly screamed like hysterical steam-engines; and Enid yelled at the full pitch of excellent lungs.

Miss Nalder was nearest, and she simply streaked up the path like a startled hare. When she reached the spot where the three girls were standing still screaming, she was horrified to find them at the other side of the fence, and very angry, too.

"What are you doing there, girls?" she cried. "Come back at once! How dare you do such a thing?"

"Corney—Corney—" sobbed Enid.

"Corney? Where?" demanded the irate mistress, just as Miss Wilson ("Bill") and Miss Lesley (known as "Bonny," from Burns's poem, "Bonnie Lesley") reached her.

"Down there," sobbed Enid; "she vanished down there."

"Shades of camp!" exclaimed Miss Wilson. "This is Jo and the leaf pit over again!"

She swung herself over the fence as she spoke, and advanced cautiously to where the children were standing.

"Mind what you are doing, Miss Wilson," called Miss Leslie. "There must be some cleft or fault there."

"What is it?" demanded Miss Annersley, who had come back to them by this time.

For reply, Miss Wilson advanced as near as she dared to the spot at which the sobbing Enid was pointing and called, "Cornelia! Are you there?"

"I've slipped," she caught in muffled tones. "Guess it's some kind of cave down here. It's a long way down, and I've banged my elbow."

"Is Cornelia down there?" asked Miss Annersley in amazement.

"Apparently," said Miss Wilson drily. "What these tiresome children have been doing, we must find out later. At present, we must see how we are to get Cornelia up to the surface."

"Come back at once, you three," said Miss Annersley; and the trio, still weeping copiously, obeyed her. They were hauled back over the fence, and dumped down unceremoniously on the path, where Anne Seymour and Vanna took charge of them, bidding them stop crying at once. The rest thronged round the fence, and looked anxiously at Miss Wilson, who was now on her knees and talking down to Cornelia. They could not hear the prisoner's voice, but they guessed that she was all right from the mistress's tones.

"Can you climb up at all?"

Apparently Cornelia replied that she could not, for "Bill" said: "What a little nuisance you are, Cornelia! I have no rope here as we had in the camp, and how I am going to raise you to the surface, I can't imagine."

There was a pause, and then she exclaimed, "You'll do no such thing? You might get lost in the heart of the mountain! Kindly stay where you are, and don't add to the trouble you are giving us all!"

Frieda took a hand here. "Miss Wilson, don't let Cornie move from where she is! I've heard Papa say that some of the caves about here lead right into the very bowels of the earth. She might get lost, and we couldn't find her. She *must* stay where she is!"

"I quite agree," said Miss Wilson grimly. "Do you hear me, Cornelia? You are not to move one step!"

She got up from her knees, and turned to the others. "And now, what are we going to do? This isn't camp, and we have no ropes to haul her out as we had with Jo."

"Should Frieda and I run up to the chalet and ask them to come?" suggested Marie doubtfully.

"How far away is it?"

"Oh, not more than twenty minutes. If we ran all the way, we should be back very soon."

"Then I think that is the best we can do.—Miss Annersley, what do you think?"

"I quite agree," said Miss Annersley briskly. "You two girls set off at once.—Miss Wilson, perhaps you will stay there and talk to Cornelia. Then we shall be sure that she

45

doesn't attempt to wander.—And the rest of you girls, form lines, and lead on to the chalet. We are nearer there than Briesau.—Miss Leslie, Miss Nalder, and Miss Stewart, will you go with them? They are not to break rank until they reach the chalet, and then they may sit down at the tables outside, and wait for us till we come."

The girls, sobered by the accident, formed lines at once, and led by Sophie and Vanna, set off at once for the alm where the chalet for which they were bound was situated. Frieda and Marie had raced off at once, and were to be seen far ahead. Miss Stewart headed the Fifth, Miss Leslie tailed them off, and little Miss Nalder acted as whipper-in at the end of the long 'croc.'

Meanwhile, the two mistresses left looked at each other.

"Are you quite safe there?" asked Miss Annersley.

"Quite, I think," returned Miss Wilson. "It's some fault in the rock, I suppose. I wonder how far down that child is?" She dropped on to her knees again, and called down: "Cornelia!"

"Yes?" came up Cornelia's voice—rather scared by this time.

"How far did you fall?"

"I—don't know. Guess it's a good way, though. Shall—shall I have to stay here for long?"

"I hope not," said Miss Wilson. "Have you hurt yourself besides banging your elbow?"

"Bruised myself a bit."

"Well, it might be worse. Don't be afraid. Frieda and Marie have gone on ahead to the chalet to get help. I expect they'll have ropes there."

"W-will they be l-long?" asked Cornelia in quavering tones. She was a plucky child as a rule, but the fall had been a shock, and it was very dark down there.

"Not very long," said Miss Wilson; "I expect they will run all the way there and back."

There was a little pause; and then Cornelia suddenly called in tones of surprise, "Miss Wilson!"

"Yes?" said Miss Wilson.

"Isn't it rummy? I can see the stars!"

"I expect you are pretty far down. And it is narrow. I have seen them from the bottom of a blast-furnace chimney in England."

"But it seems so funny seeing them in broad daylight," persisted Cornelia.

46

"That's only because you are accustomed to seeing them after dark. Are you warm? Is it damp?"

"Dry as a bone. Guess there isn't *much* rain gets in here."

"No, the bushes will act as a roof, I expect," agreed Miss Wilson.

In such chatter the minutes passed slowly, and at length a yodel told the two mistresses that rescue was on the way. A few moments later, a big peasant appeared, a coil of rope over his shoulder, and an ice-axe in his hand. After him came Frieda and Marie who were nearly out of breath with the haste they had made. He strode up to the spot with the free, easy stride of the mountaineer, and made nothing of the vault over the fence. Stepping warily, he came up to Miss Wilson, and squatted down beside her.

"Ah, das Fräulein has fallen into die Maultasch," he observed. "That is not too bad."

He unslung his rope-coil, and made fast one end to the haft of the axe which he drove firmly into the earth.

"So," he said approvingly. "We now have something to give us a hold. I will make a loop and descend, and rope the little lady. Then if you, meine Dame, and you," —he indicated Miss Annersley with a sweep of his arm —"will pull, she will easily come up."

"But what about you?" asked Miss Wilson, who doubted if she and Miss Annersley could possibly haul up this stalwart son of the mountains.

"That will be an easy matter," he said. "I shall climb, and with the rope to help, it will be easy for me. The little lady could not do it."

"She certainly could not," said Miss Wilson.

"And she's not going to try, either," added Miss Annersley in English. "She's not damaged so far, from her own account. We don't want her to sprain her ankle or break an arm!"

By this time, the man had got everything ready. He slipped the noose over his shoulders and under his arms. Then he turned to Miss Wilson. "You will please tell her to stand aside lest I should hurt her by kicking her."

Bill nodded. She stooped down again. "Cornelia! A man is coming down to you. Stand away from the opening, dear, in case he should kick you as he comes."

"I'm all right," said Cornelia.

The great mountaineer swung himself down, the two mistresses paying out the rope as carefully as they could. Presently it slacked off in their hands, and they heard him call out, "All is well!"

Two minutes later, he gave another call, and they began to pull slowly and steadily. Cornelia was a dead weight on the rope, for she was unable to help herself at all. It took hard pulling and strong pulling. Frieda and Marie wanted to come over to help, but Miss Annersley forbade it so peremptorily, that they subsided, and stood watching. At length, the top of a yellow head appeared, and then Cornelia, grimy, pale, and tear-stained, was hauled out of her hole, and set on the ground again. She rubbed her eyes with the back of her hand, and sniffed at the fresh air rather like a dog.

"Gee! That was fierce!" she said shakily, using forbidden slang in her relief. The mistresses said nothing.

"Get over to Frieda and Marie," said Miss Annersley. "Stay there till we come."

For once in her life, Cornelia did as she was told. She crawled through the fence, and then sat down suddenly on the ground.

"My legs—feel wobbly," she said shakily to the two prefects who bent over her in alarm.

"That is only the shock," said Marie sensibly. "When you have had some coffee at the chalet and washed your face and hands you will feel better. Can you stand up, Corney? The rocks are so cold to sit on."

Cornelia struggled to her feet, and leaned against Frieda, who put a protective arm round her. Then the three turned to watch the arrival of the man. He came up, helping himself as he knew how, and the two mistresses found that they had little to do but steady the rope. At length, he, too, was above ground, and then he recoiled his rope, picked up his ice-axe, and prepared to help the ladies over the fence. When finally they were all standing on the path once more, he stooped down and picked up Cornelia. Lifting her as easily as if she had been a baby, he set off up the path to the chalet, and the other four followed him meekly. At the alm, he set the child down again.

Cornelia took one or two steps, and then stopped "I'm going to be sick," she said. "I feel—"

Miss Wilson caught her in time. For the first time in her life, Cornelia had fainted.

## CHAPTER VII

## THEKLA

CORNELIA was a tough little person. It is true that she fainted, partly as the result of the shock; but she was soon herself again, and protesting vigorously because Miss Annersley was ducking her head down.

"I'm all right," she said ungratefully. "Guess I was an idiot to go off like that! I don't want anything—really."

"Are you sure you feel all right?" asked the Senior mistress doubtfully.

"Sure! There's nothing wrong."

"She'll be better when she has had some coffee," said Miss Wilson, while the man looked at them speculatively, for they were speaking in English which he could not understand. "We'd better get her to the chalet, and give her some.—Frieda, run on and ask them to make a cup of black coffee—three cups, in fact," she added, as she glanced at Miss Annersley's pale face. "Miss Annersley and I will bring Cornelia.—You run along, too, Marie, and tell them that it's all right."

The two prefects went off, and "Bill" turned to the mountaineer, and spoke to him in German. "Thank you so much for your help. The child will be well when she has had some coffee."

He nodded. "Das Mädchen has done wrong, no doubt. —Na-na, meine Dame!"—for she was trying to put some money into his hand.—"One could not leave a little one in the Maultasch, you understand."

"But we should like you to take it as a token of our gratitude," persisted "Bill." "We could not have got her out ourselves so quickly."

"Then das Mädchen shall give me a kiss," he said. "That is all the thanks I ask. She reminds me," his voice was husky, "of the little sister who went to America two years ago to seek her fortune."

Bill looked doubtfully at Cornelia, who was *not* given to kissing, and had been heard to characterise all embraces as "absolute tosh." However, that young lady was grateful to the big fellow, and she promptly lifted her face to his. He stooped down, and gave her the kiss, and then went on his way, while Cornelia, once he had gone, scrubbed her cheeks violently.

"I wish he hadn't had a beard," she complained. "He *scrubs* so!"

The two mistresses choked violently, but pretended that there was nothing wrong, and Miss Annersley pulled the child's hand through her arm. "Come along, Cornelia," she said briskly. "I expect you still feel a little shaky. You'll be all right after some coffee."

Cornelia did feel shaky, and she was grateful for the proffered arm. They went across the grass to the chalet, where, on the railed-off platform outside the house, they could see the girls waiting for them, seated round the long tables, waiting for their coffee.

"Is Cornelia all right?" asked Miss Stewart rather anxiously.

"Very nearly, I think," said Miss Annersley cheerfully. "But she has spoilt her expedition. When we have seen her elbow, and she has had her coffee, I am going to ask Frieda to take her back to the Chalet. I'm sorry to have to do this, Frieda," she went on to the prefect, "but I can't spare a mistress for it."

"I don't mind," said Frieda. "I know this walk, and have been before."

"But, Miss Annersley, I could do it, really," protested Cornelia.

Miss Annersley shook her head. "I think you could not. And in any case, you scarcely deserve it, do you?"

Cornelia went crimson. She said no more, but took her place with her own chums, remarkably subdued for her. However, she was not there long. Miss Nalder called her to come and have her arm bathed, and when the sweater sleeve had been rolled up, they found a long graze, and a bruise that was rapidly becoming black. Miss Nalder was gentle, but she was very thorough, and by the time the fomentations were over, and the wounded arm was neatly bandaged, Cornelia felt anything but ready for a long, rough scramble. Miss Annersley gave her the strong coffee, which pulled her together, and then, when a promise to do as Frieda told her had been extracted from Cornelia, the rest of the party set off, leaving the prefect and her charge to go down the mountain in their own time. Frieda was absolutely to be trusted, and the Staff felt that Cornelia had a lesson which would keep her tamed for the present. In any case, she never broke a promise, so they were quite happy about the two, since the road to the Briesau peninsula was perfectly easy.

"We go across that neck," said Miss Nalder, pointing out a kind of isthmus of thick grass, with pine-trees at one end of it. "That takes us across to the Tiernjoch group where Mechthau, the village for which we are heading, is."

"How do we get down from there?" asked Miss Annersley.

"Down to the Pass," replied Miss Wilson, who had done it about a year before. "It's a bit of a scramble, but nothing that the girls can't manage. When we did it last year, the snow was on the ground, and we had all those Juniors from St Scholastika's to handle as well. This will be quite easy."

"I should imagine so—after that," said Miss Annersley. "Well, girls, lead on.—Middles, you are not to get ahead of the prefects who will be our leaders.—Good-bye, Frieda! If you and Cornelia like to wait for the Juniors and go down with them, you may."

"Good-bye, Miss Annersley," said Frieda. "I hope you have a jolly walk."

Then, having seen the last of the Middles ahead of them, the two mistresses who had been longest in the School, and were responsible for a great deal of its organisation, set off.

Marie von Eschenau, mindful of Jo's last words, kept Thekla by her side. The two Italian girls, Vanna di Ricci and Bianca di Ferrara, walked with them, Sophie going ahead with Eva von Heiling and Anne Seymour. The rest of the Sixth and Five A straggled along after them.

"What on earth do the prees see in that *awful* girl?" demanded Margia Stevens of her own coterie.

"I do not think it is that they love her," replied Berta Hamel, sister of Sophie. "No one could."

"P'raps her own people do," said Elsie Carr thoughtfully. "But I quite agree with you, Berta. She's what Evvy and Corney would call 'a splay-footed, rubber-necked four-flusher,' and why ever she came here, I can't think!"

"And why ever you should want to quote Corney and Evvy, *I* can't think," said Margia.

"Because there isn't anything in English that will do for her," said Elsie. "It takes American to do her justice!"

"Nancy and Bill have done Corney justice all right," observed the leader of Five A. "Done out of all the fun—for this will be the best part of it—and sent home with the babies!"

"I am sorry for Corney," said Cyrilla Maurûs."—Why, what is the matter with Thekla?"

Five A hurried up to where the Sixth were all standing, Marie and Vanna arguing heatedly with Thekla, who, as Elsie said, seemed ready to have hysterics.

"What's wrong?" demanded Margia.

"It is that Thekla is afraid to cross the isthmus," explained Sophie Hamel somewhat scornfully. "She fears the narrow path, she says."

"Narrow path? *That* is not a narrow path!" exclaimed Cyrilla, looking at the six-foot ledge across which they had to go. "Indeed, Thekla, it is quite easy—See!"

And before anyone could stop her, she was racing lightly across, half-a-dozen more girls at her heels.

"Come back!" cried Marie indignantly. "You *know* you were told not to get ahead of us!"

Cyrilla came galloping back, followed by the others. "I was not doing so, Marie; only showing Thekla how easy it is," she explained.

"Oh, well, in that case we'll say no more," said Marie, who was always easily mollified. She turned to the Prussian girl. "Now, Thekla, Cyrilla has shown you that there is no danger. Come; take my arm, and we will cross together."

"I dare not—I dare not!" moaned Thekla, who showed symptoms of losing her head altogether.

"But if Vanna and I lead you—" said Marie persuasively, just as Five B and the Middles came up. "See; shut your eyes, and we will lead you across between us."

"If one of you should slip—" began Thekla.

Sophie laughed scornfully. "Slip! Girls who have been accustomed to climbing all these years slip on a broad pathway!" she said contemptuously. "Of course they won't slip. If you really are so afraid that you dare not do it, then do as Marie says—shut your eyes, and let them lead you over!"

Thekla was very proud, and the utter scorn in Sophie's voice stung her to the attempt. Allowing Marie and Vanna to take her arms, she shut her eyes, and they led her over in safety, the rest following at their heels. Sophie strolled along, Bianca and Eva beside her, all three talking busily. The two Fifths, remembering that the Staff had an eye on them, crossed sedately; and the Middles trotted over singing one of their favourite songs as they came. Up here in the mountains they were always allowed to sing if they liked, and as many of them had sweet, strong voices, the effect was good.

Once she was on the broad alm at the other side, Thekla wriggled herself free from her guardians.

"You see, it was not so bad," said Marie.

Sophie, who was passing, smiled, and her smile said things that roused Thekla's worst feelings.

"Oh, quite easy," observed the prefect. "Even the babies from Le Petit Chalet would never flinch at that."

"But if one had not a head for heights," began Vanna with the laudable idea of pouring oil on the troubled waters, "it is not easy—"

"I have an excellent head for heights," flung out Thekla. "But that narrow passage is unfit for us."

"Nonsense!" said plain-spoken Anne Seymour. "We've done far worse places than that. And if we had fallen, we wouldn't have gone far. The whole of the slopes at that part are clothed in shrubs. We might have got scratched and bruised, but that would have been all."

Thekla was boiling, but she had the sense to see that it would not do to let her fury overcome her here. She turned, and stalked after Eva von Heiling and Carla, who had gone on, and the prefects were left alone.

"Now you've made her more angry than ever, Anne," said Marie with a sigh. "It is so easy to make Thekla angry, and she does such foolish things then."

"Well, she should talk sense, then," said Anne firmly. "Don't look so upset, Marie. Nobody blames *you* for her. But the sooner she comes down from her high horse and realises that she is only a girl like the rest of us, the better for her!"

Marie looked at her thoughtfully. "Joey says that Thekla is not so much to blame as her silly parents," she said. "But it is *very* hard, Anne, after my happy time here, to have a cousin of mine like this come and spoil it."

"Well, this is only the beginning of the term," said Anne cheerfully. "You still have two terms after this. The chances are that Thekla will have settled down and become normal by Christmas. Even Stacie did that, you know."

"Yes; but Stacie wasn't anything like Thekla. She was conceited over her brains; and she thought that we ought to recognise how clever she was. But Thekla has nothing to be conceited over. She isn't specially clever; she isn't pretty; she isn't graceful. All she has is the fact that her father is Graf von Stift, and that's nothing. Besides, it is such a silly way of looking at things."

"Hear—hear!" said Anne. "But don't let's spoil a jolly walk by talking about Thekla. Tell me instead what we are going to do about Staff Evening this term."

"Joey hasn't said anything yet," said Marie. "I expect she will call a Prefects' meeting next week some time, and then we shall know."

"I smell flowers!" said Sophie suddenly.

"So do I!" And Anne elevated her nose, rather like a dog, and sniffed ecstatically. "Where can it be?"

"The flowers? From the alm near here," said Miss Nalder, passing them at this moment, with half-a-dozen Middles crowding round her. "It's full of them, September though it is."

The girls hurried on through the little belt of pine-trees through which they was passing, and as they reached its end, an exclamation of delight broke from all three. Before them lay a little wedge-shaped valley, walled round on two sides with the rock itself, while on the other were the tall black pines through which they had just come. A tiny stream ran gurgling through it, to find an outlet over the rock-wall at the one end where it was lower than the level of the valley. But what rejoiced the girls more than anything else was the wonderful display of flowers that carpeted the little dell. Globe-flowers, wild geranium, heartsease, gentian, starlike saxifrages, and clumps of purple heath lay spread before them.

"No wonder the air is so sweet!" cried Sophie. "What a treasure of bloom!"

Marie said nothing. Instead, she began to pick till her hands were filled with loveliness. Nor was she the only one. Nearly all the girls plucked till their arms were full, and their backs were aching with stooping.

"Wouldn't Jo love this?" said Marie, as she took off the ribbon that tied her curls and bound it round the flowers.

"We should never get her past it," agreed Sophie. "Oh! Look at Carla! How lovely those yellow globe-flowers look against her dark colouring!"

Marie looked round for her cousin. She was standing listlessly at one side with empty hands. The prefect went up to her. "Have you gathered none, Thekla. But you may have some of mine. I have plenty. Let me tuck some of these gentians into your tie-pin."

Thekla drew back. "Weeds!" she said scornfully. "And surely you are too old now to walk with your hair loose like that."

Marie, whose long, golden curls were floating about her in a regular Golden Fleece, laughed. "I have nothing else to tie up the flowers. Miss Annersley won't mind for once."

"You should plait it," said Thekla. "Those ringlets of yours look so childish!"

"Mamma has forbidden it," said Marie, as she pushed back the hair out of her eyes. "But I wonder if I could tuck it up into my beret?"

"Let me do it for you," said Carla, who was near them. "Will you hold my flowers, please, Thekla?"

Thekla drew back again. "You can lay them on the ground," she said.

At that, Marie suddenly boiled over. All the afternoon she had been trying to control her temper. It was very rarely that she lost it, and indeed the girls had never seen her in a rage yet. They were fated to do so now.

"You are very disobliging and unfriendly, Thekla! If this is what it is to be *hochgeborne* in Germany, then I am glad that I have never lived there! I am ashamed to think you are my cousin, and I wish you had never come here to be so unpleasant, and bring such disgrace on our family! I am not surprised that the Germans lost the War. They deserved to do so if they are like you!"

Before this torrent of words, Thekla was dumb for the moment, while the other girls gasped and stared. It had been generally decided that Marie von Eschenau did not possess a temper. Now they realised that she did, and that it was a very hot one into the bargain.

"Stacie was bad when she first came," went on Marie, "but you are a thousand times worse. Oh, Thekla, I am ashamed—most bitterly ashamed to think that you should

55

belong to our family! What Wanda would say if she knew, I do not know. She would be as ashamed as I am!"

But Thekla had recovered herself by this time, and she was every bit as angry as Marie, though her temper, easily roused, was more likely to finish sooner than her cousin's. "You are a very horrible girl, Cousin Marie! Everyone knows that if the foolish Austrians had not been so afraid, the War would have been won by us. *I* was ashamed to know that there is Austrian blood in me when my father told me—"

But she got no further. Marie suddenly seized her by the shoulders, and shook her violently. Marie was small and slight, and Thekla was big and tall, but the younger girl was no match for her cousin, and she swayed helplessly in the angry grasp, screaming, partly with rage, partly with fear.

Miss Wilson, taking big strides across the flowers, was with them almost at once, and parting them sternly.

"Girls! Have you taken leave of your senses?—Marie, I am ashamed of you! Have you forgotten that you are a prefect? Go over there to Miss Annersley at once!— Thekla, stop that absurd screaming this moment!"

Something in her tone and manner recalled the angry girls to themselves. Marie, sobbing bitterly in the reaction, fled to Miss Annersley, while Carla followed her to explain if she were allowed. Thekla, with her mouth open for yet another of those ear-piercing shrieks, thought better of it, and closed it without another sound.

Miss Wilson looked round at them. "Gather your flowers together, and get into rank," she said curtly.— "Vanna, please partner Thekla, and let me have no more of such outrageous behaviour.—I will see you and Marie this evening after *Kaffee und Kuchen*, Thekla.—Now not another word!" as two or three people tried to explain to her the cause of all the trouble, "I will hear all you have to say this evening—not before."

Miss Annersley came across the grass to her. "Miss Wilson, what are we to do? I feel like marching them all home, and saying I will never let them go another expedition unless we have the whole Staff with us!"

"I think we had better go on in files," returned Miss Wilson grimly. "I have said we will listen to what they have to say this evening."

"Very well," said Miss Annersley. "Sophie, will you

56

and Carla please lead on, and remember, you are only to talk quietly I don't know if you are trying to get our School a bad name, but you are certainly going the right way to do so."

They led out of the little valley and very little was said. It was not often that Miss Annersley sounded so stern. She was usually recognised as one of the gentlest of the Staff, while they all stood in wholesome awe of "Bill." But on this occasion, even the Science mistress could not have bettered her in strictness.

From the flower valley, they came to a broad ledge of rock, with tufts of coarse grass scattered here and there, and low-growing shrubs sprouting out of the clefts in the rock. Then they descended among pines once more, finding the short thick grass that grew here very slippery and difficult.

Evadne, who was not easily subdued, turned to her partner, Cyrilla, and murmured, "Say! We ought to try Joey's sliding stunt here, I guess!"

Cyrilla broke into delighted laughter at this recollection of a camp episode. They had all been out on a similar expedition, and, on coming to a slippery slope, Joey Bettany had forgotten her head-girl-ship, and, sitting down, had slid to the bottom, an example followed by several other people. It was just as well, perhaps, that such a thing was impossible here owing to the trees which grew about the slope. The girls slid and slithered as best they could, and not a few screams rose, as well as laughter.

At length they reached the bottom, and went along a narrow grassy path, from which they arrived once more on rock. This time, they had to climb up, and it was stiff going. The majority of the girls did not mind it at all, but two or three found it hard enough; and Thekla could scarcely crawl up the last few feet. When finally they reached the grass of another alm, she sank down, and declared that she could go no further.

"I am not accustomed to such walks," she said in her own language. "I cannot walk—no; not one step."

Miss Wilson was not in the sweetest of tempers, and this made her worse. She stood over the girl with a frown which made the more impressionable ones shiver, and demanded, "Then may I ask how you are going to get down?"

"Someone must be sent to assist me," said Thekla.

"Have you hurt yourself?"

"No; but I am weary. It is not the thing for young ladies to do—this scrambling about mountains."

"I have no doubt," said "Bill" with biting sarcasm, "that you are fully qualified to tell us what is the proper behaviour for a lady. Your own conduct has made that so evident. But I am afraid that we shall be obliged to leave you if you cannot come with us now. Perhaps, when you are *quite* rested, you may be able to crawl the short remaining distance to the village, and they will, doubtless, be overjoyed to give you any assistance you may ask."

"Guess they jolly well *will*!" whispered naughty Evadne to her partner.

"But you cannot leave me here by myself!" exclaimed Thekla, alarmed.

"I am afraid that is the only alternative to your getting up and coming with us at once," replied Miss Wilson.

She glanced across at Miss Annersley, and that lady responded at once. "Girls! Get into your files again, and lead on through those trees. We shall be at the village in ten minutes."

The girls formed ranks once more, and turned to the opening. Vanna hesitated beside her partner for a moment, but "Bill" settled her at once. "Did you hear what Miss Annersley said, Vanna? Go at once."

Vanna fled, and tacked on to Sophie and Carla, with whom she was soon discussing Thekla as hard as she could. "Bill" watched the long line of girls and mistresses disappear through the trees. Then she turned to Thekla who was still on the ground.

"And now, unless you are ready to get to your feet and come at once, Thekla, I must go."

Thekla struggled to her feet. Evening would be coming soon, and she was afraid of the pinewoods after dusk had fallen. Miss Wilson waited for her without comment, and together they went silently through the trees to the village, where the others were already congregated at the door of one of the houses; and Carla, Evadne, and Sophie were talking eagerly to the elderly woman who had come in answer to their knock.

She recognised some of the girls who had been on that memorable walk the previous year, when they had been stranded between Briesau and the northern end of the lake, owing to the breaking away of the earth above the lake. It had been impossible to go back, and it was equally impossible to hope to get round by the Scholastika end, as the path had fallen away there, too, and it was unsafe at the best of times. As this had happened when the snow was on the ground, and the frost had made everywhere slippery, the one thing they could do was to climb the mountainside from Geisalm, a tiny hamlet a little beyond what was known as "the Dripping Rock." All the Chalet Seniors and Middles had been there, and about two-thirds of St Scholastika's, the School at the other side of the lake. It had been a long, weary climb, especially as the "Saints," as they were called, were not accustomed to climbing. They had reached Mechthau at last, where they had stopped at this house for milk and a rest, and the affair had been discussed by the excited inhabitants, who saw strangers about once in six months, for weeks after it was over. So it was little wonder that Frau Schmidt was delighted to welcome those she knew, and bustled about, getting ready a great pot of hot milk, and slices of black bread, thickly spread with sweet butter.

As it was a fine day, the girls sat down on the grass outside, and ate their meal with great enjoyment. It is true the milk had a flavour all its own—consisting of onions, wood-smoke, cheese, and cream—but that was part of the fun. So was the having to share six mugs among the whole crowd of them. The Middles made rude remarks about poison, of course. As Carla said, it was only to be expected of such small children, a remark which caused those who heard it to splutter wildly, but also had the effect of silencing them.

Only Thekla drew back when Vanna passed the mug to her. "No, thank you," she said stiffly.

"You will be very thirsty if you do not," Vanna warned her.

"I do not wish any," replied the Prussian girl.

Vanna gave it up, and passed the mug to Elsie Carr who was waiting. But her words came true, for foolish Thekla felt on the way down that she would have given anything for a drink. Miss Annersley would not allow her to drink from the mountain streams, so she had to do without, and was moved to wonder inwardly how castaways at sea managed when they had to go without water for hours on end.

When the girls had finished, Miss Annersley paid their

score, and they set off on the last stage of their tramp. Across the alm, towards a rough path bordered by pines they went, followed by the entire population, who chattered at express speed in their own patois about the young ladies. This was not a difficult path, as Miss Wilson knew from experience. It was rocky, and they would have to look out for hidden tree-roots and boulders; but the daylight would last till they had reached the bottom, and were on the Tiern Pass, and after that, it was as easy as walking across the playing-field would be. But before they began the scramble, Miss Annersley, with a keen eye for the weaker members of the party, halted them, and proceeded to rearrange the party. The youngest girls were each given an older guardian, and Margia Stevens, Violet Allison, Maria Marani, and Cyrilla Maurús, who were none too strong, were bidden join the prefects, who took one between two of them. Finally, she glanced at Thekla. By this time, the girl was so really tired, that she was wondering how she would ever get back to School. All unaccustomed to healthful exercise, she had felt the strain of this expedition severely. Miss Annersley was annoyed enough about the scenes she had made; but she was a very humane person so she beckoned Louise Redfield and Thora Helgersen to her. They—the two biggest girls in the Sixth, strong, and used to such tramps—came at once.

"Girls, I want you to look after Thekla," she said quietly. "She is tiring now, as she is, of course, unaccustimed to such walks. Give her an arm down." Then she added with a smile, "I don't think anyone will be sorry to hear that we expect the hay-carts on the Pass. I rang up the School just now, and Matron said she would send to August Stein and his brother-in-law, and ask them to meet us at the bottom of the path. Now, are you all ready? Then lead on."

They set off, and Thekla found that her two sturdy supporters helped her considerably. They scarcely spoke to her, but in any case, they needed all their breath for their work. In one way, it was not so hard as that slippery grass slope, for it was rough going; but they had to climb more than once in order to avoid the great boulders which the autumn and winter storms had rolled into the path, and this made the way longer. But at length they were at the bottom, and there were the two hay-waggons awaiting them. Even Thekla found nothing to say about riding in such a thing, though on another occasion, she would certainly have expressed herself indignantly. As it was, she was too thankful to climb in, aided by a good "boost" from Louise, and sink down on the boarded floor. Then they rattled along the Pass, and over the meadow-land to the gate in the playing-field. It was hard work to roll out again, and go across the field, for their muscles had stiffened while they had been sitting, but it was done somehow. And once they were in, they found that Matron had prepared for them. Everyone was ordered off to a hot bath, and then desired to anoint herself with some of "Matey's" special liniment before she dressed again. After that, they streamed down to the Speisesaal, where *Abendessen* was awaiting them, and even Thekla found that she was so hungry, she could have eaten dry bread.

The Staff were merciful that night, and did not insist on the usual Saturday night dancing. The girls lay about with books and needlework till the bell rang for bedtime, and a long, sound sleep soon put most of them right by next day.

There were two people, however, who were not so happy as they might have been, for Marie and Thekla had to go to the Staff and hear exactly what Miss Annersley and Miss Wilson thought of them and their behaviour. It was a rare thing for quiet Marie to be in trouble; and Thekla had never heard such home-truths before in her life. Cornelia, it had been decided, had punished herself sufficiently, so nothing was said to her. But the Staff drew long breaths of relief when the evening ended and they could be sure that all their charges were safely in bed and asleep.

CHAPTER VIII

## THE PREFECTS IN COUNCIL

"WELL, all I can say is that I think you've done yourselves proud!"

"Joey, do you really blame me?" Marie von Eischenau turned an incredulous face to her friend.

Joey shook her head. "Not altogether—though I must

61

say it wasn't exactly in keeping with prefectorial dignity for you to *shake* the little wretch. Still, she deserved all she got. Only, I rather wish you had kept it till you were safe in the School grounds. It's a blessing that most of the visitors have gone, and that that is rather a deserted place. There aren't two in a thousand who ever find it out."

Marie had coloured during this speech. She knew quite well that it had been a childish thing to do. "I—I lost my temper," she said. "Oh, Jo! I *have* let us down!"

Jo's eyebrows flew up at the slang. "Hullo! Where did you pick that up? Not from me; I've been talking like an Elsie book all this term—the fruits of being head-girl," she added with a laugh.

Marie joined in her laugh rather shamefacedly. "I must have picked it up somewhere. I will try to be more careful, Jo. I know Madame does not like us to use slang."

"Oh, it isn't forbidden," said Jo. "Well, what has happened to Thekla?"

"Mademoiselle had us in the study, and lectured us," said Marie. "I do not know what she said to Thekla, for she had us separately. And Miss Annersley and Bill had us up before that. They were both very angry."

"I can't see the Abbess being really *angry*," said Jo.

"She was! She made me feel—"

"Rather a worm?" suggested the head-girl as Marie stopped short for lack of something that would express her feelings adequately.

"Yes; that just describes it. She is never annoyed with us; and she spoke so gravely."

"Far as that goes," said Joey, "I can't understand *you* losing your temper like that. I always thought you hadn't any at all."

"I don't mind small annoyances," said Marie gravely. "I think it was because I was already so ashamed of her. And then she was so rude to Sophie and Carla!"

"H'm! Yes; that will have to stop. We can't have silly, snobbish ideas of that kind in the School. The babes might pick them up, and it's the last thing any of us want. I must say, Marie, I see your point. And Sophie has been here as long as any of us; and is one of the best we have."

"Yes; and then to think it was my own cousin!"

"We can't help our relatives. *They* are foisted on to

62

us whether we like them or not. It's friends we have to choose; and you choose jolly well."

A little silence followed this last pronouncement. Jo was trying to see what could be done to alter Thekla; and Marie was turning over what Jo had said in her own mind. While this was happening, the door opened, and Frieda Mensch and Simone Lecoutier came in from an extra coaching in mathematics.

"What has happened to Bonny Leslie?" asked Frieda, as she laid her books down on the table.

"How d'you mean?" asked Joey, dismissing the problem with relief.

"Why, she is so dull—"

"She is sad," pronounced Simone weightily. "There was no smile about her. And she never noticed when I copied a sum down wrongly."

"H'm." Jo was suitably impressed by this phenomenon. "There must be something the matter. Bonny never lets the least slip pass!—*I* know that only too well," she added ruefully.

"Perhaps she is not well?" suggested Marie.

"It is not that kind of sadness," said Simone. "It is as if she had heard some bad news."

"I hope not," said Joey. "Well; when are the rest coming? I said half-past fifteen, and here it is—twenty to sixteen, and only us four here!"

"Sophie and Carla were having Latin coaching," said Frieda. "Vanna had a music lesson at half-past fourteen, so she may still be with Herr Anserl."

"Poor Vanna! Every day I am more and more grateful that everyone decided that it would drive Vater Bär mad if *I* went to him," said Jo. "I love him out of lessons, but in them—"

"He *is* cross," agreed Marie, who had had one term with him and then had gone to Miss Denny, because all her lessons had been spent in tears on her side and raging on the irritable old Music master's.

The sound of running steps broke in on their conversation at that moment, and then Carla and Sophie, with Eva von Heiling, raced in, and tossed their books down anywhere.

"I am sorry we are late, Joey," cried Sophie. "Charlie kept us such ages over some Livy we *could* not understand!"

"Oh, well, so long as you've come," said Jo easily. "I suppose Vanna will come shortly—if there's anything of her left to come," she added as an afterthought.

"She was putting away her music as I came upstairs," said Eva.

"Then let's sit down. We haven't too much time; but I daren't take anything out of this evening. It's my turn for prep duty, and you know how much of your own work you can get done with those Fourth Form imps."

"Corney will be subdued, at least," remarked Frieda. "She has been very good all the week so far."

"That's why I'm anticipating trouble tonight," said Jo pensively. "It always means a bad outbreak with her."

"For once, I believe it's the result of the shock she had," said Frieda. "We told you that she fainted when it was all over."

"Ye-es; that may be. It isn't like Corney to faint, is it? I shall hope for the best at that rate. Anyhow, if they do start any monkey-tricks, I have something that will squash our one and only Corney at once."

"What is that, my Jo?" asked Simone. "I should like to know something that would keep her in order."

Jo looked round them. "I may tell you all so long as it goes no further," she said. "My sister told me when I was up there at the week-end. It's just this: if Corney behaves herself this term, she's to go into Five B after Christmas. She should have been promoted with the rest—she's quite old enough. But they decided to keep her down another term and see if the disgrace would steady her. Mademoiselle will tell her to-night, and if it *doesn't* calm her down, it ought to."

"It will," said Marie with conviction. "She was very sorry to be left behind when all the others were promoted. Also, she is almost fifteen, and the others in that form are not more than fourteen. I know she had felt it though she has said nothing."

"How do you know?" demanded Jo.—"Hullo, Vanna! Finished at last?"

"Herr Anserl kept me so long over my Bach," complained Vanna as she sat down beside Sophie. "I am sorry to be late, Joey."

"All right," said Jo. "We haven't begun yet.—Go on, Marie. How do you know?"

"I saw her face when the lists were read out," said Marie, "and she looked as if she would cry at first."

"Then let's hope this will make her pull up," said Jo. "All right, Vanna. I've just been telling the others that if Corney behaves herself this term she is to go into Five B after Christmas. Now let's get to work."

"What shall we take first?" asked Frieda.

"I think the Staff Evening," said Jo. "We should have settled it last week, really. It doesn't do to leave it too late. Besides, we want to get in first with our invitation. Now then, everybody, ideas, please!"

Needless to state, this bland invitation dried everyone up. As Marie said presently, it was asking too much to plunge them suddenly into anything like that when they were still talking about Cornelia.

"Come along," said Jo when the silence threatened to become permanent. "What do you suggest we should do to entertain our preceptresses?"

"Our what?" demanded Sophie from the other end of the table.

"Preceptresses—in other words, our mistresses. Let's be original if we can! So please don't suggest a dance, a play, or a series of competitions. We've had all those *ad nauseam*."

"I wish you would not drag Latin into it," sighed Carla. "We have had an hour of Livy already—"

"Then it ought to come naturally to you," retorted Jo. "Wake up, you people! What are we to do to entertain the Staff?"

"When do you think we should have them?" asked Simone.

"Doesn't that rather depend on what we do? If we want to make it an open-air affair, we ought to have it fairly soon. I don't mind telling you, my children, that this weather won't last much longer. According to some wonderful man we heard over the wireless on Saturday night, there is to be a severe winter when it starts. This is October. It may hold up to the middle; but that will be as much as it will do. Remember, we are much higher than in the towns.—What did you say, Frieda?"

"I only said we were rather more than four thousand metres above sea-level," returned Frieda, looking slightly ashamed of herself.

"Exactly. Well, we always get snow sooner than they do

in the valleys. So if we make it an outdoor affair, it will have to be on Saturday as I said."

"But that is so near," complained Vanna. "We shall have no time to prepare anything, Jo."

"No; that is true," agreed Simone. "To-day is Tuesday, and the bell will ring for *Kaffee und Kuchen* before very long. It leaves us no time, my Joe."

"That's what I thought," said Joey. "Then you all agree that it had better be an indoors affair?"

"I do, for one," said Sophie. "And I have an idea. Let us have it as near Hallowe'en as possible, and give them a Hallowe'en party."

The idea was greeted with cries of joy.

"Sophie! But what a good idea! Of course we must!"

"And we can do such funny things!"

"I say! I hadn't thought of that! So we can! We'll make them all duck for apples—with their mouths—in a tub! Oh, *won't* it be priceless!"

"And sit before a mirror, brushing their hair and eating an apple with a mirror before them to see their future husbands," supplemented Frieda.

"And they can do that thing Evvy told us of last year."

"What was that, Marie?"

"Don't you remember? Jumping over twelve lighted candles, one after the other, to see how many happy months they will have."

"We must buy chestnuts and roast them. We play a game in France," said Simone. "One takes the two halves of a walnut shell, and puts in one a paper with one's name on, and in the other a paper with that of a friend. Then one lights the tapers—"

"What tapers?" demanded Marie.

"The tapers in the shells, of course."

"You never told us so," said Frieda. "But what happens next?"

"One lights the tapers, and floats them together in a tub, blowing gently till they reach the other side without the tapers going out."

"What happens if they do?" asked Jo.

"Then it is a sign that your friendship will die as the light has."

"And supposing they *don't* both reach the other side?"

"That, too, means the same thing. If one sinks, then she whose name it bears will be the one to break the

66

friendship. If both sink, then there is a bad quarrel."

"It wouldn't be bad fun," said Jo thoughtfully. "And there is the Three Plates game."

"That we played last year? That would be very funny."

"And I've just remembered a be-yew-tiful one, done with an apple and a burnt cork!"

"What is it, my Jo?"

"Show you when we decorate."

"Then it is settled?" inquired Frieda.

"Oh, I think so," replied Jo. "But, now that I come to think of it, I don't believe we could find a suitable date in the neighbourhood of Hallowe'en—some of the Staff are heavily engaged about that time. But it wouldn't matter if we postponed it for a week or two—we'd have more time to prepare. Anyway, we'll make it good fun for everybody, even the babies. We can begin at six, as they have to go off at eight; and leave all the worst things till they've gone. I don't believe," said Jo solemnly, "that it would be good for them to see *all* the things we can think of!"

There was an outburst of laughter.

"I don't believe it would," agreed Marie, when they were grave again.

"Sure it wouldn't! Simone, will you write the invitations? You are the best of us when it comes to scribbling."

"Very well," said Simone.

"But why not let us spend a little time and paint them each one?" suggested Marie.

"Then you'll have to do without *my* help," declared Jo. "After what happened last week in drawing. I'm having nothing more to do with it."

They all chuckled. Jo, never good at art, was always a trial to Herr Laubach, the short-tempered drawing-master who came up one day in the week from Innsbruck to teach at the School. At the last lesson, Jo, who had wakened that morning in a bad temper, had lost her patience, never very great, and had done her level best to annoy him. She had dropped her rubber, broken the points of her pencils; dug the lead so deeply into the paper that there were no hope of rubbing out wrong lines —which were plentiful!—and had made such an appalling mess of the freehand design he had given her, that he had lost his head, and picking up pencils, rubber, and paper, had flung them at her. At the same time he had vowed that she was too utterly stupid to continue; whereupon Jo, very much on her dignity, had risen and left the room. What was more, she had refused to return. And when the infuriated man had stalked off to Mademoiselle with the whole story, that lady informed that, since Jo was such a persecution—it was his own expression—she had better stop the lessons. She could do extra mathematics in the time. Exit Herr Laubach, partially appeased!

To Jo, Mademoiselle had merely said that since she could so far forget herself as to behave like a baby, it would be advisable for her to stop her drawing lessons. Instead, Miss Leslie would give her extra preparation in mathematics in which she was weak. As Jo hated mathematics as much as she loved English, no one could say that she had not got her deserts for once. Hence the laughter at this recollection.

Jo had got over her first annoyance about the matter, so she merely grinned amiably, and got up from her seat. "If you all like the fag of doing it, I shan't stop you. Most laudable, I'm sure! There's the bell, and we've got to go now. This meeting is hereby declared closed."

"Well, that is one thing settled," said Marie as she watched the others hurriedly put their books away, "but I wish—I *wish* that Jo had said how we are to reform Thekla!"

## CHAPTER IX

## THE SENIOR MIDDLES IN TROUBLE

THE Middles of the Chalet School could generally be counted on to keep things lively. So far, they had behaved themselves remarkably well this term. Perhaps the fact that four of the leaders had been moved up to one or other of the Fifths may have had something to do with it. However that may be, the first four weeks of the term had, with the exception of the trouble with Thekla, been unusually quiet. That being the case, it was high time for them to do something. As Joey Bettany had sagely remarked, it was not to be expected that they would reform all at once like that.

The outbreak occurred the week after the last prefects'

meeting. The news of the Staff Evening had kept them in check till then, and that was longer than the Chalet School had known peace in all its career before.

The immediate cause of the first event was the School clock. For the last week or two it had been losing time. As the lesson bells were all rung by it, and as most of the Staff had never finished when the bell rang for Break, one or two lazy people complained about it. The bells for the beginning of School and the end of Break were rung according to the watch of the prefect on duty. When the people who came immediately after these continued their lessons five and ten minutes after the watches of their pupils told them time was up, it gave those young ladies a good excuse for grumbling.

"I'm tired of this!" announced Margia Stevens, head of Five A. "We've been docked of nearly ten minutes' Break this morning—and for *algebra*!"

"And our essay lesson was more than five minutes too long," added Berta Hamel, who was *not* gifted in languages.

"Guess the old clock's wrong," said Cornelia, who was with her friends even though her School position should have relegated her to the other end of the room.

"Tell us something we don't know!" retorted Elsie Carr. "That doesn't make things any better!"

"Should we tell Mademoiselle?" asked Ilonka.

"No thank you! She's been rather—trying, ever since the row with Thekla and Marie, and she'd most likely tell us to mind our own business." Thus Evadne Lannis. "Can't we do something to the wretched thing ourselves?"

"Such as what?"

"Well, what about putting it on?"

"And have someone find out, and a fuss? Not me!" said Margia simply.

"Well, what *shall* we do, then? Would it be any use appealing to the prees."

"Not an atom; so you may make up your mind to that," declared Elsie Carr.

"We can't shove it on," said Margia slowly. "They'd be sure to guess. But suppose we try to put it right ourselves."

"But we could not," said Cyrilla, who was not very quick.

"Couldn't we? I have a book on how to make things; I

believe it tells you there how to make a clock. Half a minute, and I'll fetch it." And Margia jumped up from her seat, and raced off to her locker. She returned presently, hugging a thick volume, and sent Cornelia to ask for a certain volume of an encyclopedia which she thought might help.

"What shall I say if Sophie asks me why I want it?" demanded Cornelia.

"Tell her you want to read about clocks, of course," said Margia. "She won't think of *making* them; she'll think you want to get up their history."

Cornelia vanished, and presently came back, laden with the required volume, which she dropped on the nearest table. "Come on, Margie! What do we do?" she said expectantly.

There was silence in the Common Room for the next half-hour, while the party carefully digested all the information they could gather on a clock's interior working.

At length, Margia looked up. "There doesn't seem to be anything too complicated about that," she said. "I think we'll be able to manage all right."

"But when are we to do it?" asked Ilonka.

"In prep. So we'd all better get to work and get prep done at once."

There was a good reason for this decision. The lights in the big room used by the two Fifths for preparation had fused that afternoon, and till the electrician could get up from the "Stephanie" to attend to them, the room would be in darkness. As it was doubtful that the man would get to the Chalet before *Abendessen*, Miss Annersley, after a consultation with Mademoiselle and Miss Wilson, had told the girls that they must take their preparation to the chemistry laboratory. Miss Wilson had arranged to lock up all chemicals, and to turn off the gas at the main. When that was done, the mistresses felt there was nothing left with which the girls could get into mischief. The "Chemmy Lab." was built out from the Chalet at one end, and so was quite away from the rest of the School. Miss Wilson, who might have otherwise bothered them, was enjoying her "Free" day, and they had heard her say that she was going up to the Sonnalpe for the afternoon and evening. They knew she had gone, for Elsie, returning from a music lesson, had overheard Mademoiselle giving her a message for Mrs Russell. No other member of the Staff was likely to worry about them. They were Fifth Form girls, and, as such, could be relied on to get through their work quietly. The only danger, so far as they could see, was that one of the prefects might come for something. However, that had to be risked.

It was arranged that Elsie and Margia should get the clock down and take it to the laboratory before *Kaffee und Kuchen*, and the rest were to do prep in every spare moment. As the bell rang for games just then, it was not until they had all come in from the playing-field, fresh and glowing, and had hurried upstairs to change into the simple frocks of brown velveteen with cream muslin collars and cuffs which were their usual evening wear, that the Fifths were able to do anything. It caused a positive sensation through the Sixth when Louise Redfield, running into the Common Room, nearly fell over Cyrilla Maurús who was reading what proved to be the Duruy *Histoire Française*.

"What on earth are you doing prep for now?" demanded Louise when she had saved herself from falling, while Cyrilla picked up her book which Louise's hurried entrance had knocked out of her hands.

"I was reading it," said Cyrilla with all the dignity she could summon to her aid.

Louise stared at her and gasped. "Since when have you become studious?"

"We are at a very interesting period," said Cyrilla primly. "I find it delightful reading."

Louise said no more. But she went over to Joey Bettany to ask if she knew if Cyrilla were quite well.

"Far as I know she is," said Joey, staring. "Why?"

"Because she's reading French history."

"Well, there's nothing wrong in that. I do it myself."

"Oh—you! But then you aren't Cyrilla. You know as well as I do that she's almost invariably at the bottom of her form."

"P'raps she's turning over a new leaf," said Joey idly. "Anyhow, I can't interfere with the kid because she likes to swot up history. There's nothing wrong in that."

Louise was squashed, and said no more. Meanwhile, Cyrilla, warned by what had happened, left the room, and ran upstairs to pass on the warning to the others. The result was that most of the Fifths were late for their afternoon meal, since they had stayed in various form-rooms to work. However, they had done a good deal, and they hoped, by going straight to preparation after *Kaffee*, to get the rest done in plenty of time.

By half-past eighteen all prep had been done after a fashion, and Margia and Elsie, armed with torches, went off to the Five B form-room to get the clock.

It is, perhaps, unnecessary to say that they had *not* taken Thekla into their confidence, and she had not begun her work at the same time as the rest, as it was her turn to practise till eighteen. She had only been at her prep half-an-hour, and she was seated at a bench, a little away from the others, with her back to them. She took no notice of them, and they took none of her.

Presently, the two ambassadors returned with the clock, and a fine time began. They took it to pieces, carefully putting all cog-wheels and screws into a deep box, so that they should not get lost. As a good start, they *boiled* the lot, Hilda Bhaer having observed that she had heard of one of her sailor uncles doing this. Then they got dusters from a drawer, and dried and dusted every part. Evadne Lannis, who had silver toilet things, had brought down the polish she kept for them, and everything was polished. After this, they began to put it together again. It was a hard task, but they stuck at it, and at length got every cog and every screw in *some*where.

All this time, Thekla had been hard at work on French history, German essay, geometry, geography, and repitition. The clock was finished just as she laid down her pen for the last time, and just as the bell rang for *Abendessen*.

"There! It's done!" said Margia, regarding their work with pride. "It's clean, at any rate!"

"Let us hope it will also go well," added Giovanna Rincini. "When do you put it back, Margia?"

"After *Abendessen*. Elsie will come with me and the rest of you must keep the Staff and the prees so busy they can't come and catch us. I'll wind it up in the morning. I don't suppose anyone will bother about it to-night."

Thekla overheard all this, but she was not interested, and thought no more about it. She gathered up her books and papers, and left the laboratory, followed by the others.

By the time they had put their books away, and got to the Speisesaal, the rest of the School was sitting down to soup. Luckily for them, however, Mademoiselle only said, "I suppose you did not hear the bell."

Margia and Maria Marani, as the heads of the two forms, went up to her, and apologised, and she said no more, merely remarking that it was a good thing the usual room would be ready for them on the morrow.

The rest of the scheme worked very well, and when Margia had got up at six the next morning, and slipped downstairs to wind up the clock and set it going, they dismissed the subject from their thoughts. The sequel came when they were all in the room, waiting for the bell for *Frühstück* to ring.

From the next door room, they heard the chiming of the clock.

"Eight o'clock," said Joey casually. "*Frühstück* is late this morning." She spoke in German, which was the official language for that day; but her next remark was in English.

The conspirators had grinned at each other at the sound, for most of them had felt rather dubious as to the efficacy of their methods, and this familiar sound had reassured them. But when the clock had struck eight, it went on. What was more, it was not the ordinary chime, but something quite different. There was a grim, do-or-die ring about it that forced the sound on the notice of everyone.

"Great Caesar's bathmat!" exclaimed Jo in forbidden English. "What's the matter with the clock?"

She fled to the next room, followed by the others, and they all stood staring at the clock which went on striking as if it meant to split its sides in the effort. The Fifth, if anyone had noticed them, looked scared. They had not bargained for this. But nobody did notice them. Everyone was occupied in staring at the clock as if it had suddenly dropped from the ceiling; and the clock itself was striking away in a manner that threatened to end its career for ever. Jo's jaw had dropped in amazement; Elsie's eyes looked ready to start out of her head; Frieda and Simone were clutching hands; and Cornelia, screaming with laughter, was trying to keep count of the strokes, and failing ignominiously.

On this scene, entered Mademoiselle; and a very angry Mademoiselle. The bell for *Frühstück* had rung twice already, and no one but the Staff who had come from their quarters at the other end of the house, had turned up.

She had come to seek her flock, and, guided by the laughter that arose from them, she had found them. "What is the meaning of this?" she began in angry German. The next moment she too was staring, transfixed at the clock, and wondering what in the world had happened to it.

It was at this moment that Thekla suddenly remembered the half-heard conversation in the laboratory the night before.

"*You* have done this, Margia!" she exclaimed. "You were playing with the clock last night in the laboratory!"

As Margia said, that put the fat in the fire with a vengeance. As, at the moment Thekla spoke, the clock suddenly stopped dead, having chimed two hundred and seven times—so someone computed—her tones carried far, and Mademoiselle heard every word.

The two Fifths were told that, after *Frühstück*, they might go to the study, and then Mademoiselle marched the School into breakfast without another word. The worst came later. Mademoiselle, having heard their story, had condemned them to paying for the repair of the clock which had finished going when it had finished striking, and left it at that. But the prefects had them up later, and told them all exactly how babyish they had been, till they were all reduced to a wormlike feeling. Then they were told that they deserved to be sent to Le Petit Chalet where the babies were. After that, Joey let them go. With one accord, they went in silence, and waited till they got to their form-room.

Arrived there, Margia promptly rounded on Thekla. "You rotten sneak!" she cried. "Of course you had to go and tell tales!"

"Just like her!"—"Wish she had never come here!"— "Horrid little wretch!"—"Pie-faced, splay-footed—"

The last remark, Evadne's, was promptly squashed by Margia, who interrupted her with, "*Stop* that horrid expression! It's simply disgusting!"

"But—but—I don't understand!" stammered Thekla, who had never thought of getting anyone into trouble by her remark.

"You understand well enough," said Elsie Carr, a hard look coming into her pretty face. "You told tales to Mademoiselle and the prees, and we are going to have nothing to do with you! We don't like sneaks *here*!"

In vain did Thekla protest that she did not understand.

74

The two forms had—most unfairly, as it happened—made up their minds that what she had done had been done deliberately. They turned their back on her, and, for the rest of the day, she found that she was sent to Coventry with a whole-heartedness common to most of the exploits of the Quintette, as the set led by Margia and Elsie were known. Even Joey had queried the new girl's intention when she had spoken. However, the prefects had decided, after discussing the matter, that Thekla had been surprised into it, and let it go. But that was not much help to Thekla.

## CHAPTER X

## HALF TERM AT THE SONNALPE

It had been arranged that the Half Term should be spent up at the Sonnalpe. Many of the girls had little sisters up at the Annexe which had been opened that term for delicate children, and only a few of them had seen it. Besides, Juliet Carrick and Grizel Cochrane, two old girls of the School, were in charge, and this was another attraction to those who had been at School with them.

"I think it will be simply topping," said Evadne, who had recovered from the clock episode, and was her usual insouciant self again. "When do we go, and how? Are we to walk up?"

"We Seniors in the Sixth are," said Carla. "You younger girls will go up the new coachroad in coaches."

At the beginning of the summer, a new road had been opened from the western side of the Sonnalpe. This new road had been built to make it easier to get patients up to the great sanatorium which was the centre of life "up there," as the girls called it.

"I do wish I had not promised Wanda I would spend Half Term with her!" wailed Marie von Eschenau. "Now you will all see the Annexe before I do!"

"You're coming up the week-end after Staff Evening," said Joey consolingly. "Wanda would hate it if you didn't go. And you must tell us all about little Kurt. I'm longing to hear how he is getting on."

"Well, I wish Friedel had been a doctor," returned Marie. "Then Wanda might have been living up there like Gisela. How many of you are going to 'Das Pferd,' by the way?"

"Maria and I, of course," said Frieda.

"Naturally. You're Gottfried's sister, and Maria is Gisela's."

"Corney, Bianca, and Cyrilla come with us," went on Frieda.

"And Paula and Margia and I go to the Annexe," added Sophie.

"What about 'Die Rosen,' Jo?" called Eva von Heiling across the room.

"Evvy, Elsie, Lonny, and the two Merciers come to us," replied Jo.

"Mean you're having Evvy, Elsie, and Lonny together? Isn't that a risk?"

"Not with my sister there," replied Jo with a chuckle. "*She'll* keep them in order all right! No messing about with clocks when she's in charge!"

"Guess you're—" began Evadne; then she suddenly remembered that the prefects were there in full force, and shut her lips firmly.

"Well?" said Jo teasingly. "Go on! What am I?"

"A mean! Yes you are, to go on teasing Evvy like that!" cried Margia, rushing to the defence of her friend.

" 'Mean' is an adjective—not a noun," said Jo sententiously.

"I've heard you use it as either!"

Jo suddenly relented. "So you have. Well, there's not much time left—only two days. What a gorgeous time we shall have!"

"Rather! If only the weather keeps like this, it will be wonderful!" put in Frieda.

Jo glanced out of the window at the sun which was blazing down, regardless of the fact that it was the end of October. "It simply isn't natural! We've never had an autumn like this before. The weather will be breaking soon, and when it does, it will be something outrageous in the way of storms."

"It will be a bad winter when it comes," remarked Frieda quietly.

"How do you know?"

"Have you not noticed the berried trees and shrubs?"

"Of course I have. They are simply scarlet this year! I never saw such a wonderful year for berries and nuts—cones, too."

"Well, that is a sure sign. Nature provides food for the birds and squirrels against the time when there will be nothing else. Have you not seen how the squirrels are gathering all day and every day? They are laying up great stores somewhere."

"It's rather wonderful," said Jo thoughtfully.

"Everything God does is wonderful," replied her friend.

The bell rang for *Mittagessen* just then, and they had to get into line to march into the Speisesaal. But for the rest of the time, the coming exeat filled their thoughts to the almost entire exclusion of work. Even Simone, who was working hard with a view to entering the Sorbonne the next year, became *distraite* and careless; and Joey made such a disgraceful exhibition of herself in algebra, that Miss Leslie very nearly told her to go out of the lesson and stay out!

At last the day came, and from first thing in the morning the School buzzed with excitement. Lessons that morning were more or less of a farce. They ended at eleven, luckily, and the Staff were merciful, and passed over mistakes with a leniency which would have been amazing at any other date.

A good meal awaited them, and then they set off. The girls who were going home, together with those who would go by the coach-road, were to walk down to Spärtz, the little town at the foot of the mountain. The rest—twelve girls, together with Miss Stewart who was to escort them there—would walk round the head of the lake, and climb up by the mountain path. She would go on to the hotel at the Sonnalpe after she had left the girls at "Die Rosen," taking with her those who would be at the hotel, too.

Meanwhile, up on the Sonnalpe, all was bustle. Madge Russell was wandering through the bedrooms prepared for the girls, to make sure that everything was as it should be, while her husband was following her, grumbling at every step at the coming of the girls, to which he was looking forward as much as his wife, though he would have scorned to say so.

"They will be here in another half-hour," said Madge when they were downstairs again in the great salon.

Jem Russell groaned in answer to this remark. "Only

77

another half-hour before the enemy are on us? What have we done to be treated to this?"

Madge laughed. "Don't be so absurd, Jem! You know perfectly well that you are looking forward to it as much as I am."

"Maynard and Humphries have the best of it," said the doctor enviously. "Lucky fellows! They can go and bury themselves at the Sanatorium. I've got to stay here to play host and keep a hand on the reins, and see that they don't quite kill you!—Was that the 'phone?"

"Yes, dear. Go and answer it, and come back in a better mood."

He got up from his chair and stalked off to the telephone, whence he presently erupted violently into the room.

"Madge—quick! Get that bag I left on the office table! I'm wanted at the San.—urgent op.—thank goodness Jack Maynard is there already!"

Madge fled through the french windows, and down the garden to the office, where she picked up the bag lying on the table, and tore back to the house with it to find her husband hastily shoving various articles into his pockets. She gave him the bag, and he snatched it and hurried off, his thoughts far remote from her. Madge went back to the great salon where they had been, and glanced round once more to see that everything was ready for her guests. She was having more girls than she had expected at first, for Dr Jack Maynard and Captain Humphries, secretary to the Sanatorium, who usually lived at "Die Rosen," had offered to go to the great building further down the alpe, so leaving their rooms vacant.

"The girls will love to come here," said Madge, as she put up camp-beds. "Also, I don't want to have to put anyone with Stacie."

"Just as well," her husband had agreed. "Stacie is getting on too slowly for my liking, and I would rather know she could be alone when those young hooligans get obstreperous."

She was thinking over all this, when the sound of a motor-horn, tooting violently and unmelodiously in the distance, told her that the first consignment was almost on them. She ran out into the hall to greet them. Just as she reached the door, she remembered the babies—her own little son, and the twin children of her own twin brother, Dick—and called up the stairs for them. They came flying down—that is, the twins did. Baby David followed more sedately in the arms of his little nurse, Rosa. He shouted delightedly when he saw his pretty mother, and nearly flung himself out of Rosa's arms to get to her.

"Twins, stand here beside me," directed Madge rather breathlessly, for her son was tugging at her hair, and gurgling joyously. "Don't dare to move till I tell you, Rix! Take Peggy's hand!"

Then she went to the door, regardless of the fact that Rix had stuck his hands firmly in his pockets, and was following his little sister with an air of manly independence which would have convulsed his uncle had he been there to see it.

The first coach had just driven up to the door, and was discharging its load as Madge opened the glass screens and appeared on the step, followed by the children.

"Girls, I'm delighted to see you! Welcome to the Sonnalpe, all of you!"

"They couldn't wait to see you," explained Miss Wilson as she descended from the coach, and came to shake hands with the ex-Head. "I knew you wouldn't mind if we came straight here, and they can walk back to the hotel. They have only light cases to carry. What a big boy David is getting!—Have you forgotten me, Davy boy?"

David was, like his mother, friends with all the world, and he was quite willing to be hugged and kissed, not only by Miss Wilson, but by the girls too. When he was finally returned to his mother, he was tumbled and tousled and looked as though his tiny tunic had been worn all day instead of having been freshly put on only half-an-hour before. Then the girls turned to the three-year-old twins. Peggy was as ready with her kisses as Davy, but Rix was on his dignity and drew back.

"I'm a boy; boys don't kiss," he said stoutly.

"Who told you that?" demanded his aunt.

"Well, I never sees Uncle Jem kiss any girls—'cept only you, an' Jo, an' Peggy," retorted the young man.

"I told you not to speak of your aunt as 'Jo,'" said Madge, thus countering an unanswerable remark. "And if people offer to kiss you, Rix, it is very rude to refuse it."

79

"Will ve girls want to kiss Uncle Jem?" demanded Rix with deep interest.

He got no answer to *that*. Smothering a laugh with difficulty, Madge turned to the girls again. "Sophie, I think you and Margia and Paula had better not linger here too long. You are expected at the Annexe, you know. At least three people are longing to see you again, if not more."

"We'll go there now, Madame, since we've seen you," said Sophie cheerfully. "Come, Paula and Margia.—You are all coming down after tea, are you not, Madame?"

"Yes. Tell Juliet to expect us this evening as soon as possible," said Madge. The girls picked up their cases, and hurried off, and after a little more talk, Frieda led off her contingent to "Das Pferd," the home of her brother, Gottfried Mensch, and his pretty wife. Miss Wilson marched hers down to the big hotel at the other side of the Sanatorium, accompanied by Miss Leslie and the second coach load. This left "Die Rosen" with only Evadne Lannis, Elsie Carr, Ilonka Barkocz, and the two French sisters, Yvette and Suzanne Mercier.

Madge began to send them to their rooms. "Evvy, you know your room—it's the one before Joey's. You and Lonny are together.—Elsie, you and Yvette and Suzanne are just opposite. I must stay here to welcome the rest when they come. What time did they start?"

"Half-an-hour after us, Madame," said Elsie.

"Then they won't be very long."

Madge picked up her son from the settee where she had dropped him, and tucking him under her arms, sauntered out to the gate to see if she could see anything of the walkers. Just as she got there, she heard a shout, and she saw Joey, with Simone hanging on to her arm, leading the van, while Frieda, Carla, Vanna, and Bianca came next.

"Hullo, you people!" called Madge. "Where are the rest?"

"Gone straight to the hotel with Charlie," replied Jo, who looked wild in the extreme. She had taken off her beret, and stuffed it into a pocket, and her hair was standing on end as though she had carefully brushed it up for the occasion. But she was brown and healthy, with a glow in her cheeks called there by the exercise. Madge, noting all this, felt, for the hundredth time a sudden rush of thanksgiving that they had come out here. As a small child, Jo had been terribly delicate; now she was as sturdy as heart could wish. She had reached her sister by this time, and was seizing on Baby David. "Give me Davy!—Well, old chap, you are *growing* all right.—He won't be a baby much longer, my dear!" This last to her sister.

"No; but he'll be a boy," retorted Madge. "I'm glad to see you people. Bianca, you are going to Gisela's, you know, with Frieda?—Frieda, *dear!* Where is your pretty hair?"

Frieda took off her beret, and slowly revolved, so that Mrs Russell might admire the arrangement of the long plaits swung round her head in a coronal. "I am nearly eighteen, you know, Madame, and Mamma said I must put them up. This is the easiest way when one has so much hair as I."

"It's very pretty," said Madge, with a wistful look. "But it seems to me that I must be getting very aged when a girl who was one of my Junior Middles comes to see me with her hair up."

"Frieda is not the only one," cried Carla. "Vanna has hers up, now; and Bianca's goes up after Christmas."

"Oh, dear!"

"Well, at least you can console yourself with the thought that mine can *not* go up," laughed Jo. "Carla, aren't you going to the hotel? I'd better go and show you the way."

"And we must go, too," said Frieda. "We shall be late for *Kaffee* otherwise." She pulled her beret over the plaits. "Are we coming here before we go to the Annexe, Madame?"

"Yes; all meet here.—Yes; you can go with Carla if you like, Jo. I don't want her to wander about the alm half the evening! Hurry back, though."

"I shan't be long," replied Jo, putting on *her* beret. "Come on, Carla."

They went off, and Madge returned to the house. Master David, at nearly eighteen months old, was trotting all over. He was a big, solemn boy, with his mother's dark eyes and curls, and a square chin which gave him a startling resemblance to Rix who had elected to resemble his Aunt Madge, while Peggy was as fair as her brother was dark, and a gentle, peaceable little soul, who was completely at the beck and call of her masterful twin. The pair were still in the salon where their aunt had left them, and were engaged in playing with Rufus, Joey's magnificent St Bernard, who considered himself the chosen guardian of the small folk.

"If you two make yourselves dirty, you'll have to go and ask Rosa to wash you," warned Madge, who, now that her own small son was running about, often felt that she wanted six pairs of hands and three pairs of eyes at once.

The twins got up. They saw no sense in having more washings than they could help. Also, Elsie and Evadne had come down, and Peggy and Rix were wildly excited about "vese big girls," as Rix called them. The pair were accustomed to the people from the Annexe. They adored Robin Humphries, and they got on quite well with Stacie Benson when she was able to be with them. But they had never mixed with such crowds of big girls before, and they were looking forward to it with great glee. Neither twin was troubled with shyness, so they were soon making friends, and when Jo arrived on the scenes, having first gone upstairs to make herself fit to be seen, she found that her niece and nephew were very much at home, and climbing all over the strangers. Evadne, who was an old friend, they scorned for the moment.

"Where's Jem?" asked Joey as she sat down and took her nephew on her knee.

"Gone to the Sanatorium.—An urgent operation call," said Madge. "Well, Simone," as that young lady came into the room, "aren't you longing to see René again? Why, my dear girl! What *have* you done to your hair?"

"I am growing it, Madame," replied Simone. "When I go to the Sorbonne, I wish to put it up, so Maman bade me let it grow. It has not been cut since last term, and soon I shall be able to turn it up."

Madge groaned. "What with you and Frieda and Vanna, I shan't have any of *my* girls left shortly!"

Vanna laughed, and touched the coils of plaits over her ears self-consciously.

"How is the Annexe doing, Madame? Is Juliet a good Head?"

"Excellent," replied Madge.—"And Grizel is managing the music very well. She had to go to Spärtz this afternoon for a lesson with Herr Anserl, so she won't be back till this evening as she has to walk both ways."

"That's the worst of the train stopping," said Jo.

82

"Yes; it finished for the season last Saturday," said Madge. "It's gone on nearly a month longer than usual, you know."

"And the steamers have not finished till to-day," said Vanna. "What a good autumn we are having!"

"Winter will be all the worse when it comes," said Jo pessimistically. "And this heat is *awful* in November! I believe we shall have an earthquake before long."

"Nonsense, Jo!" said her sister. "Jem says we are right out of the earthquake zone here."

"Does he indeed? Then how do you account for the awful one they had in 1670 when nearly all the houses in Innsbruck, Hall, and the Unterinnthal fell down? And there was one the century before; hundreds of people died in that."

"Are you sure, Joey? I haven't heard of them before," said Madge sceptically.

"I'm sure all right. I've been reading Tirolean history lately—it's tremendously interesting. I was struck with the earthquake business because *I'd* always thought we were well out of it. But what happened before can happen again, and this weather really is uncanny at this time of year!"

Vanna laughed. "You are very gloomy, Jo. I expect, though, we shall have nothing worse than a bad thunderstorm or a blizzard."

"A blizzard up here?" observed Simone. "Oh, suppose it was so bad that we could not get back to Briesau for many days!"

"Thanks! I'd rather be excused," said Mrs Russell decidedly. "That would be likely to mean short commons for all of us. If there were a blizzard, it might be difficult to get supplies up, even by the coach road, and with forty-five extra people, rations might prove rather a problem."

"It would be an adventure, though," said Jo hopefully.

"One I'd rather not experience, thank you. We'll hope that nothing so trying will happen. And now, tell me what you have all been doing this term. How is the Hobbies Club going?"

"Very well," said Simone, one of the prefects responsible for the running of the club. "Jo has cut out several new puzzles, and also some brackets and pipe-racks. Marie is learning to paint on china, and is doing some cups and

83

saucers for the Sale. And the others are doing various things, too. We mean to have a big sale this time, Madame. The Saints are also busy. And do not the girls at the Annexe work, too?"

"Yes, indeed! We are going to have an Annexe stall to ourselves, and amaze you with our supplies. So you'll have to work if you want to beat *us*!" laughed Madge.

"Jolly!" said Jo appreciatively. "Well, what else do you want to know? The Guides are going strong, of course. We've arranged the Guide Tests as usual, though Bill—I mean the Captain is as squashing as usual if we try to take more than three in a term. It's rather—confining!"

"I'm glad she does. Some of you people have no idea of moderation, and would work till you were ill or silly if you were left to yourselves. And now, Joey," went on Madge, rising as she spoke, "give me my boy, and ring the bell for *Kaffee*. The twins are to have it with us to-day for a treat."

Jo handed the baby over to her sister. "There he is!— Go to Mummy, Davy boy.—Twinnies, come here and let me see you! You haven't spoken to me, yet."

Peggy scrambled up from the hearth where she had been winding a harness of coloured wools round Rufus, and ran to her younger aunt, her angelic little face lifted for a kiss. But Rix was careful to keep at arm's length.

Jo promptly made a grab at him, and hauled him up to her. "Now then, monkey, what's the meaning of this?"

"I'm a boy," said Rix defiantly. "Boys *don't* kiss, Auntie Jo. I'm not goin' to!"

Jo chuckled. "Don't see how you can help it," she said; and solemnly planted a kiss on either cheek, much to the indignation of the "boy."

Rix hit out valiantly at this outrage on his dignity; but Jo was prepared, and easily defended herself. Madge had to come to the rescue in the end. Taking Rix by the arm, she walked him over to the other side of the room where she left him with Vanna, and then returned to her sister. "You ought to be ashamed of teasing him like that, Jo."

"Not a scrap," returned Jo promptly. "He's my nephew, and if I can't kiss my nephew, who can I kiss?"

"You'd better attend to your English," said her sister severely. "Peggy, take these twists, darling, and hand them round."

While Mrs Russell poured out the coffee for the girls, with milk for the twins and David, Peggy trotted about with the wicker basket containing the twists of fancy bread beloved by the girls.

"Why isn't Robin here," asked Jo suddenly when they were all busy with their *Kaffee und Kuchen*.

"We are to bring her back with us from the Annexe tonight," said her sister. "She begged to be allowed to stay there till you came, so that she could welcome you herself."

"Is she stronger, Madame?" asked Simone anxiously.

The Robin—otherwise, Cecilia Marya Humphries— had been the School baby for a long time. She had been brought to the School shortly after the death of her mother from the white scourge which the Sonnalpe doctors were fighting, and had quickly become the adored pet of the whole School. But with her mother's dark loveliness, the Robin had also inherited delicate health, and the previous term had been one of great anxiety about her. She had shown some of the symptoms of the disease, and they had been very much afraid lest anything should go wrong with her. However, these were passing off, and had only been the outcome of her rapid growth. Still, the girls could not forget how worried they had been in the spring and early summer, and all listened eagerly to Madge's reply.

"Robin is much better, Simone. She is thriving up here, and has gained all she lost in the early part of the year. But she is going to be tall like her father, and she isn't a baby any longer now."

"Is Uncle Ted all right?" asked Joey, referring to Captain Humphries.

"Very fit; and quite happy about the Robin now."

"Good-oh!—Mercy, Rix! What *are* you doing?"

She might well ask. Master Rix, bored with the conversation, had descended from his seat, and was engaged in trying to turn a somersault.

He turned right side up at Jo's question, and turned. "Standin' on my head," he said sweetly.

"Well, kindly behave yourself properly at meal-times," said Madge, "or I will send you from the room."

"*She* does it," said Rix pointing aggrievedly at Evadne, thereby making that young lady blush violently and choke into her coffee.

"Who's 'she'?" demanded Jo.

"The cat's mother," said Rix calmly; whereupon both his aunts fell on him in horror.

"Rix, where did you learn that? Don't let me hear you say it again!"

"*Rich-ard Bettany!*"

Rix looked supremely satisfied at the sensation he had created. "I heared Dokker Jack say it," he explained.

His Aunt Madge settled him at once. "Doctor Jack is a man, and may say lots of things a little boy may not. Remember what I said, and don't say it again, please."

Rix subsided, and the meal went on quietly. Towards the end of it, Vanna asked about Stacie Benson.

"Is Stacie at the Annexe, Madame?"

Madge shook her head. "No; she hasn't been there much yet. She is poorly to-day, and Dr Jem wouldn't let her come downstairs. She is in her room—at the other side of the house.—By the way, Jo, she wants to see you after *Kaffee*. You might run up for a few minutes when you have finished. Don't stay long, though. We shall be going to the Annexe very soon; and besides, I don't want Stacie tired. This hot weather is trying her very much."

Jo drained her coffee and stood up. "I've finished now, so may I go at once? I expect she'll have a good deal to discuss about the mag., and I have some contributions I want to give her."

"Very well. Run along; but remember, whatever you do, don't overtire her."

"I'll be good. Poor old Stacie! This *is* hard luck!" And shaking her head over Stacie's condition, Jo went off first to her own room to get the contributions for *The Chaletian*, and then to go quietly across the long corridor which led from one side of the house to the other, and so to Stacie's room.

<br>

CHAPTER XI

## THE STORM

STACIE BENSON lay on a long, narrow invalid couch near the window of the pretty room which had been specially fitted up for her. It was a very dainty room, with white walls on which were hung copies of Margaret Tarrant's paintings. A tall white bed stood in the centre of the room, and on one side of it was a table which had shelves for the invalid's belongings. A smaller one was between her and the window, and on it stood a big blue bowl, full of late roses. Down one side of the wall was a set of low book-shelves, laden with all Stacie's precious books, and at the other was a pretty dressing-table. Rugs of pale blue lay about the polished floor, and Stacie herself wore a loose frock of blue. Her fair hair was bobbed like Jo's, with a deep fringe which suited her, and she lay on rose-pink cushions. The last time Jo had seen her, she had been almost sitting; but to-day she was nearly flat, and there was no colour in her cheeks.

Joey stood in the doorway, and hailed her cheerfully. "Hullo, Stacie! I hear you want to see me. I want to see you all right. My dear, I've brought you this pile of con-tributions for the mag., and we'll have to go over them together some time this week-end."

Stacie turned her head. "Oh, Joey, I'm so glad to see you! How long have you been here? Come and sit down, won't you?"

Jo shut the door behind her, and flopped the great pile of manuscripts on to the seat of a wicker chair which she carried over to the side of the couch, setting it carefully down, so that when she was sitting, she faced the invalid. Then she bent down and kissed the pale girl lying there before she picked up her papers, and dumped them down on the table.

"There you are, my love! Those ought to keep you busy for a while! But I say? You're flat again! Madge said you weren't well, but I didn't know you were down. Is your back bothering you?"

"Just a little. It ached rather badly all day yesterday, and I didn't get much sleep last night, so Dr Jem said I'd better have a day almost flat and not come down at all. I was rather bored, because I'd been looking forward to seeing you all; but it can't be helped. I'll sleep to-night, and then I'll be all right tomorrow. It doesn't happen often now, Joey. But they think it's this hot weather. I do loathe it! It makes me feel so sticky and tired. But I really am getting on now."

"It *is* hot," said Jo, who had settled herself comfortably. "Did you ever know anything so weird as this heat we're having? Here we are into November and the thermometer is soaring like a lark! It might be August!"

"I wish it would get a little colder," sighed Stacie. "Madame thinks it will end in a thunderstorm, and then we shall have winter all in a hurry."

"I suggested an earthquake," said Jo with a grin. "I say, what a shock we'd all get if the house suddenly began to rock!"

"I thought we were far away from any fear of that?"

"So did I till I read Josef Egger's *Geschichte Tirols*. Then I found we weren't."

"Well, I hope you are wrong, Jo. I should hate an earthquake. I don't mind thunder—I never did! But I should loathe it if my bed suddenly began to swing about!"

"I shouldn't exactly like it myself," confessed Jo. "Well, what about all this lot?"

"What a pile! We never get as much as this, surely? And I have heaps from the Annexe for their pages."

"Oh, we generally get plenty—especially this term. But I must say we've done rather well this term. I'm glad the Annexe are making a good start. Now, look here, Stacie! We don't want too much of anything. I've sorted these out, and put them into separate pile. These are essays. I wouldn't have more than three. These are stories and legends, but be careful you don't repeat anything we've already had. I sent you up the copies of the past numbers, and they're all indexed, so you'll soon see if anyone is being lazy, and simply using something that's been done. These are poems—a very mixed grill! Corney sent in some appalling limericks. I've left them—they'll make you yell with laughter. But I don't think we'll take them, thank you! Evvy has evolved some conundrums. I haven't had time to look them over, as she only gave them to me this morning, so you must. And whatever you do, blue-pencil anything outrageous. You know what Evvy can be —even being moved up to Five B hasn't done much for her in that way. Besides, I believe the entire tribe had a hand in them.

"These are Marie's Games Notes; here are the Notes of the Clubs. Bill sent this for the Guide Pages—thank goodness everything for that has to go in to her first, and she makes the selections! That's two pages off our shoulders, at any rate! These are the general School Notes. I've done those, and I think they're all right. But you might just skim them through and see I haven't made any silly mistakes in spelling. You know what I am, and there was a good deal to do this term. You might add something to the Games Notes about Marie being a splendid Games prefect. She wouldn't put it in herself of course, and it *ought* to be in! She's better even than Grizel was, and she was very good. Marie has more patience, though; and she spends a lot of time coaching backward people, which is more than Grizel ever did. If you were an ass at games, you might whistle for all the interest Grizel was ever likely to take in you!"

"I don't believe that ought to go at the end of the Games Notes," said Stacie thoughtfully. "Doesn't Marie sign them? Then it simply can't go there. I'd better put it on the Editorial Page, don't you think?"

"Good idea! I hadn't thought of that. You're right, of course."

"Very well, then; I will do that. What are you people going to do this evening?"

"I believe we are going to see over the Annexe. Robin is coming back here with us, you know. She's sleeping with me—and Simone."

"I knew that. She was full of it last Sunday. You'll see a change in her, Jo. She's getting tall, and she looks a real little schoolgirl now."

"She'll still be my baby, though," said Jo sturdily.

"In that way—yes. She is very pretty, Jo."

"She always was, bless her! What are *you* going to do!"

"Stay here till Nurse comes from the San. to get me to bed."

"Alone? I say, would you like me to stay with you?"

Stacie laughed. "Don't be silly, Joey dear! It's topping of you, but I shall be quite all right. Nurse won't be long, and once I am in bed, I shall probably go to sleep. So it would be keeping you for no purpose. You go with the rest to the Annexe and bring the Robin back. She's dying to see you, you know."

"Well, if you're quite sure—"

"Of course I'm sure! Now tell me the latest Middles' row."

Jo crossed her knees and clasped her hands round them. "They've been quite quiet for them this term. This last week has been the worst." And she began to tell Stacie the story of the Fifths' attempts at clock-repairing.

The story was just finished when there were shouts of! "Joey—Joey! Buck up—we're waiting!" and she had to go. On the way downstairs she nearly fell over the nurse who was coming to get Stacie back to bed, and had to stop to apologise. Luckily, Nurse was a good sort, and she merely chuckled comfortably over it.

"I'm rather solid," she said. "You'd have had your work cut out to upset me. Don't go back to Stacie to-night, will you? She's tired, and ought to have a long rest if she can get it."

Jo promised, and then ran down and out into the garden where the rest were awaiting her impatiently.

"What on earth have you been doing, Jo?" asked her sister. "We called you ages ago!"

"Trying to slay Nurse," said Jo with a chuckle. "I nearly fell over her on the stairs, and I simply had to stop and apologise."

"I should think so! Well, come along!" And Madge walked off with Simone and Vanna, while the rest followed in groups of three or four. They had just started, when Mrs Russell suddenly turned round.

"Joey, where's your blazer?" she asked.

"In the cloaker. I don't want it, surely! It's simply boiling hot!"

"I think it will probably rain before we get back," said Madge. "Everyone else has hers, and you must have yours. Don't be silly, Jo, but do as I tell you without any more argument."

Grumbling under her breath, Jo went back, and presently returned with the despised blazer over one shoulder. Then they set off for the Annexe, where Juliet and Grizel met them on the steps of the verandah.

"Welcome to the Annexe!" cried Juliet, a tall, fair girl, with very dark eyes and a commanding manner. "It's splendid to have you all here at last! Come in! We're longing to show you round!"

Grizel Cochrane, just returned from Spärtz and a somewhat trying music lesson, nodded her prettily shingled head to one or two, and then made for Jo. "You've seen all over it before, Joey. Come upstairs and have a chat with me."

"Can't," said Jo. "Where's my Robin?"

Grizel shrugged her shoulders. "Oh, I forgot her. She's somewhere about." And she walked off by herself. She wanted to see Jo for a chat, and she was rather inclined to be jealous of the other girl's warm love for little Robin.

Joey looked after her with a grin, and then ran in at the open door, calling, "Robin—Robin! Where are you, my Robinette?"

There was an answering cry of "Joey!" and the Robin ran out of a near-by room, right into Joey's arms, and the big and the little girl hugged each other ecstatically.

"How you've grown, Baby!" said Joey at length, holding the small girl at arm's length from her, and scanning her with loving eyes.

It was a charming little person that she saw. The Robin had lost all her baby chubbiness, and was a slim little girl of ten, with a mop of black hair, curling all over her head. Deep brown eyes smiled out of a rosy face as lovely as a little stray angel's, and dimples dipped in the corners of the pretty mouth. The two were a great contrast, for Jo's black locks were straight to lankness; and her eyes were black and twinkling, while she had never in life been able to lay claim to a dimple. They went off together quite happily, and talking both at once in French which was the Robin's mother-tongue.

It was only a short visit they paid the Annexe that time. Madge, with an anxious eye on the heavy clouds that had come up after sunset and shut out the moon and stars, allowed the girls time to go round the rooms, and then hurried them off. It was so dark that they were obliged to use electric torches to show them the way, and she felt nervous till she knew they were all safe. For this reason, the people from "Die Rosen" accompanied those at the hotel to their abode, and then raced back to the big chalet beyond the Sanatorium. The fears troubling the lady communicated themselves even to placid Vanna, who felt thrills going up and down her spine as she raced along, Simone's hand in hers, at the heels of the ex-Head and Joey who had the Robin between them. They got under cover safely, and were standing in the hall, getting back their breath, when the whole place was suddenly lit up by a vivid flash of lightning, and almost at the same moment the thunder pealed and crashed overhead like a battery of guns firing simultaneously.

Joey, who had been leaning negligently against a tall stand on which was a bowl of chrysanthemums, jumped violently, overturning the stand, and sending the bowl and flowers to the floor with a crash which startled the rest almost as badly as the thunder.

"So it's come," she said when she had recovered herself. She looked down at the bowl pensively. "I say! I seem to have bent that bowl rather. It's in fifty pieces!"

Madge, who had jumped even more violently at Jo's effort than at Nature's, merely nodded, and ran upstairs to the nursery to see that the little ones were all right; but they were all sound asleep. It was otherwise with Stacie, who had been awakened out of a light slumber by the fearful peal of thunder with which the storm had broken. She was lying wide awake, watching the play of the lightning across the black skies. She turned her head as Mrs Russell entered the room.

"All right?" asked Madge in matter-of-fact tones.

"Yes; quite, thank you, Madame. What a magnificent storm! Isn't that lightning marvellous?"

"Very," agreed Madge. "It will rain soon, I think. I'm going to close your windows, my dear, or else you may have a flood. Shall I send someone up to sit with you?"

"Isn't Rosa in the nursery with the babies?"

"Yes. And the Robin will be coming soon. She is to sleep in Jo's room, you know, but it's too early for our *Abendessen*, and that would be too late for her. Rosa has her milk and bread and butter waiting, and she will be tired with all the excitement, so I shall send her up as soon as I go down."

"Then I shall be all right," said Stacie confidently.

"Are you sure, dear? It's not like having someone in the room, you know."

"No; but I never really mind storms. The only one I ever hated was the one in the spring when I got hurt. And I shouldn't have minded that if I hadn't lost my head. Are the babies asleep still?"

"Sound as tops—every one of them.—Why, what's this? *The Chaletian?*"

"Yes; Joey brought me this pile to choose from. With all we have from the Annexe, we ought to have a thick magazine this term, oughtn't we?"

"That's splendid," said Madge warmly. "Oh, did you hear that minor crash just now—after the first peal of thunder?"

"Yes, I did. What was it?"

"Jo knocked down the stand in the hall with that big blue and yellow bowl of mine on it. I liked her description of the affair!"

"Oh, what did she say!" asked Stacie eagerly.

"'I seem to have bent that bowl rather. It's in fifty pieces!'" repeated Madge with a laugh.

"That was one way of describing it! Do you mean that big one I loved so, from Tiernkirche? Oh, I'm so sorry! I always liked that bowl—it looked so clean and fresh! What was Jo doing to break it?"

"Leaning up against the stand. She jumped when the thunder came, and that did it!"

"Well, it was rather sudden, that thunder. Anyway, it's better than that earthquake she's been prophesying with such gusto. To hear her, you'd think it was the one thing she'd always longed for."

"If we had an earthquake, Jo would be sick," declared her sister. "She's no sailor in a stormy sea. With a tossing earth, I should think she would be done."

"Poor old Joey!—What's that—hail?"

"Only rain," said Madge, going to the window to look out. She might have saved her trouble. The rain, threshing wildly down, completely obscured the panes with a curtain of streaming water. "It must be coming down wholesale!" she exclaimed as she began to pull the curtains together, having switched on the electric light which, for a wonder, had *not* fused. "I can't see anything for rain!"

"This will be the end of the hot weather," said Stacie with a sigh. "I'm thankful for that, anyway! We'll have a hectic winter, shan't we? It's been delayed so long."

"I hope not. There, dear; now you are snug! Would you like a drink before I go?"

"No, thank you. I don't want anything at present. I shall go to sleep again presently. You know, Madame, I feel heaps better already. It's so much cooler. I believe it's been the heat, just as Dr Jem said, and not my stupid old back at all."

"Quite possible," said Madge, with a tender smile at the girl who was taking her hard sentence so pluckily. "We want you up for Christmas, you know. I must go now, Stacie. The others will be wanting me, and Robin *must* come to bed. If I don't drop in later myself, I'll send Jo to see what you are doing."

"I'll be sleeping," said Stacie with decision. "I can't keep my eyes open now. It can thunder till it's blue in the face if it likes. It won't disturb *me*!" And she snuggled down on her thin pillow, shut her eyes, and was as sound asleep as the three babies before Mrs Russell had left the room.

"What a change!" thought Madge as she went downstairs to capture the Robin and send her off to Rosa. "Who ever would have thought that that impossible little prig, Eustacia Benson, could have become the nice girl, Stacie, that she is to-day? And in so short a time, too!"

"Madge!" Her sister's voice brought her back to mundane things. "I say, Madge! Jem hasn't come back yet, and I rang up the San., and they say he'll probably be there all night. The op. is safely over—it was sudden appendicitis—but he wants to stay till the poor lamb comes out of the ether.—Well, what are you giggling at so madly?"

"Your expression," choked Madge.

"What's wrong with it?"

"Oh, I didn't mean your face!" Madge pulled herself together. "The patient, my dear Joey, is a disgustingly fat old man who *will* persist in overeating himself, in spite of all that anyone can do. He's been staying at the hotel, but Jem was called in two nights ago to prescribe for him, and said if he went on as he was doing this *must* come. And to hear you calling that bald-headed old *glutton* 'poor lamb' was too funny for anything!" Madge got up. "Where's Robin? She must go to the nursery and have her supper."

"Aren't *we* to have any? I'm frightfully hungry."

"Yes; but it won't be quite ready yet. Take Robin upstairs for me, Jo, and leave her with Rosa. I'll go and hurry up Marie with the *Abendessen*."

Madge disappeared down the hall, and Jo went to call the Robin and take her up to Rosa, who promised to sit with her till she fell asleep. Then Jo ran down to the salon.

The girls, who had been left to amuse themselves, were engaged in playing "Statues." This is quite a good game for a few. If there are too many people it becomes complicated. Evadne took each girl by the hand, and swung her violently round, letting go at the top of the swing. The idea is to stand exactly as you are left without moving a muscle until the one who has done the turning has gone round, inspecting, and given her decision as to which is the best. As Evvy had disposed of them all in sundry positions, she was going round, making comments calculated to cause giggles from the "statues."

"My, Simone! What a face! You look like a gurgle on that old cathedral of yours in Paris—"

"Like a *what*?" demanded Joey at this point.

Evadne turned round. "Oh—you!" she said. "I said 'a gurgle'—you know; one of those things that sit on the roof all hunched up, putting its tongue out at you—"

"I did *not* put my tongue out!" cried the outraged Simone at this. "I am not a rude baby to do such a thing!"

"And if you mean *gargoyle*, I'd say so!" added Jo calmly, "and not talk about architectural ornaments as if they had something to do with *brooks*!"

"Stop arguing, children!" Madge suppressed all three. "*Abendessen* is ready, so come along. I don't suppose the thunder will affect your appetites."

"Guess not mine," said Evadne cheerfully.

Jo slipped a hand through her sister's arm, and they led the way into the Speisesaal, where a truly holiday meal awaited them. The amount they all ate made Madge gasp with horror.

"Girls—girls! Has Mademoiselle taken to starving you at School? I never met with such appetites in my life!"

"Everything is so jolly good," explained Elsie Carr, holding out her plate for a second helping of fruit trifle. "We always get heaps to eat at School—but this is different. Besides, the thunder has made *me* hungry."

Jo surveyed the table. "There seems to be a scraping of jelly left in that bowl," she said thoughtfully. "Seems a pity to waste it, doesn't it?"

Simone promptly passed the bowl to her, and she set to work to clear up what was left of the jelly. When they arose, there was little left on the table but the china and silver and flowers. They went back to the salon, but either their good supper had made them sleepy, or the storm, which was still raging, had affected them. At any rate, they were all sleepy, and when their hostess suggested bed, they went without a murmur, even Evadne having nothing to say. By ten o'clock, they were all sound asleep, regardless of the thunder which was going round and round the lake as it frequently does in this mountainous district, growling itself out. Indeed, it was four o'clock when the storm was dying away in the distance, and Dr Jem let himself softly into the house. The rain was still pouring down, but there was an iciness about it that told the doctor it would soon become something much colder, and winter would begin in earnest. He stole up the stairs on tiptoe, having removed his boots in the hall, for fear he should awaken the girls. He peeped in at the Robin and Stacie; then went off to bed, where he was soon sleeping as soundly as any of them, and never stirred till his usual rising hour, seven. Then he merely grunted and rolled over again, aware that Gottfried Mensch was in charge at the Sonnalpe now, and he could sleep in peace for another two hours.

CHAPTER XII

## WINTER BEGINS

THE girls slept late. Madge considered that it would be just as well to let them sleep as long as they could, and told Marie, the head of the domestic side of "Die Rosen," that no bells were to be rung nor gongs sounded until nine o'clock. The consequence was that it was ten before they had finished breakfast. Then Joey got up, and strolled to the window. "Who ever would have thought of *this* coming on top of the thunder?" she remarked, waving her hand towards the view.

Simone who had followed her, nodded her little black head sagaciously. "It is late this year," she said. "This is the fifth day of November.—Why, Joey, what is the matter?" for Jo had given a sudden wild yell.

"The Fifth of November—Gunpowder Day! Oh, how long does anyone think this wretched snow will keep going? We simply *must* have a bonfire!"

"Why, pray?" demanded Madge. "If you want to say things about poor Guy Fawkes—"

"Oh, I don't! Anyhow, people were idiots to say he hid in cellars under the Houses of Parliament when there weren't any there. Besides, *would* the gunpowder of that time have been strong enough to do it?" She addressed this question to her brother-in-law, who shook his head.

"Doubtful, I think, Joey. It was a very crude affair—nothing like the high explosives we have nowadays. In

96

any case, if he hid under the House of Commons, as we were told when we were small, he'd have had no chance to blow up the King and the ministers. What the writers of history all seem to have forgotten is the fact that there is only one known case of the King going to the House of Commons—namely, when Charles I went to arrest the five members and found that 'the birds were flown.' No; I think we can discount a good deal of the old legend."

"Just as we've discounted the story of Alfred burning the cakes, and Canute telling the waves to go back," murmured Joey, who, nevertheless, entertained some private doubts as to the accuracy of detail in Dr Jem's remarks.

"Exactly. Well, I don't want to depress you, but I'm afraid you won't have any bonfire to-night. That is going on for the rest of the day, or I'm much mistaken!" He nodded to the window, through which was to be seen a wild dervish-dance of snowflakes. The rain overnight had changed to hail early in the morning, and that had become snow by eight o'clock.

"You can amuse yourselves in the house," said Madge consolingly. "We can play battledore and shuttlecock in the hall this morning; and there is the billiard-room for those who want to try their hands at billiards. Robin, I think you had better go to the nursery and play with the twins and David. I know Peggy has some splendid game she wants you to try. This afternoon, we'll have dancing and a sing-song; and what about tableaux for this evening?"

"Oh, Madame, that will be splendid!" cried Vanna. "Only, what about the others? Will they be able to come?"

"I am sending Andreas down to the hotel to tell them all to come up. He will bring them along, and they can't come to grief with him. Dr Gottfried will fetch the crowd from 'Das Pferd,' too. I'm afraid the people at the Annexe must satisfy themselves where they are. It's too wild for them. Now if you've all finished, we'll ring the bell for Moidl to clear away and then you can get to work."

"That's the best plan," said Dr Jem. "Stacie is better this morning, so Nurse will dress her as soon as she comes, and then we'll get her into her chair and bring her downstairs. She will be in that little room off the stairs, and not more than two of you at a time may go to her. Remember, she is still far from well, and I don't want her thrown back."

"Can't I go up to her till Nurse comes?" demanded Evadne.

"Yes; run along. But don't be too noisy."

Evadne made a face at the doctor before she darted out of the room, and Joey rang the bell. Half-an-hour later, Nurse came to attend to Stacie, and then she was lifted into her invalid chair, wheeled to the lift which Dr Jem had had installed, and brought downstairs, and rolled into the little room which was kept as a sewing-room. The back of the chair was lowered till the invalid was resting comfortably, and then Joey came in to see about *The Chaletian*. She herself had been editor until the previous term, when she had become head-girl. She had wisely decided that she could not do both things properly, so the editorship had been turned over to Stacie, and she had done very well. The discussion of the various contributions kept the pair busy for the rest of the morning, as Madge Russell was glad to note when she peeped in at them at intervals.

Vanna and Carla went to the billiard-room, where they were presently joined by the Seniors from the hotel, and they had a fine time, knocking about the balls. Dr Jem groaned for his cloth, but the girls were careful, and did no harm. The Middles were soon hard at hide-and-seek all over the house, the nursery and the Den being forbidden ground. By degrees, the Seniors forsook the billiard-room, and wild shrieks of laughter and shouts of dismay soon echoed through the chalet. Madge herself was busy in the kitchen, and had promptly chased away the first pair who had gone there for shelter. The Staff, from the hotel, were happy in the salon which the girls, by one consent, left alone.

"Guess there's too many finnicking bits of smashables about," was how Evadne phrased it.

And all the time, the snow came dancing down as if it never meant to stop.

"Guess we're going to be buried this time," said Evadne at *Mittagessen*. "And say! Don't that wind howling sound like a lot of old witches and fiends and things trying to get at us?"

"Rats!" retorted Cornelia Flower. "There aren't such things as witches."

"Guess you think you know everything," retorted Evadne in return. "What about the Brocken where they hold Witches' Sabbaths? The Devil sits on the top, and they all dance round him and worship him, and—"

"Shut up, Evvy!" interrupted Jo. "You're scaring the babes."

Violet Allison and Greta Macdonald, two very nervous Middles, really did look rather pale. Greta, in particular, having come from the Scottish Highlands and lived all her life among people who had dozens of legends about kelpies, and the Dark Folk, and black hares, was shivering at Evadne's suggestions. There was no mistress at this table, as Jo and Simone and Frieda were there, so none of the elders knew what was being said. However, Jo was squashing enough, and Evadne relapsed into silence.

"Do we all sing this afternoon?" asked the Robin, who was sitting at Jo's right hand, and beaming happily because she had her beloved Joey next her.

"Not immediately," said Jo with a grin. "I doubt if any of us could after this meal. But later we will. Before that, we'd better get our tableaux fixed up."

"How do we manage about clothes?" asked Frieda.

"Use what we can. We'll manage all right. Curtains— and safety-pins, and brooches, too."

"What pictures shall we do?" asked Simone.

"We'll discuss that after *Mittagessen*. My sister wants us all to rest for half-an-hour, so we can arrange it then. The Staff aren't to have anything to do with it. We're running it ourselves, and they can be audience."

"Will they be our only audience, Joey?" asked Paula von Rothenfels, who with Margia Stevens and Sophie Hamel had come up from the Annexe.

"Marie and Co. from the kitchen department, of course. And any of the doctor's people who like to face the storm. We'll ask to have *Abendessen* early, and then we can have our tableaux after, and take as much time as we like."

"Well, I think it sounds very jolly," said Frieda.

They carried out their plans, and while they were all supposed to be lying down after the meal, they discussed the tableaux and everyone argued at the top of her voice. Finally, it was all settled, and then they were called to the salon, where Madge sat at the piano, and all sang songs until sixteen o'clock, when *Kaffee und Kuchen* came in.

Madge had agreed that *Abendessen* might be at seven so that they could take the time after for their performance.

The doctor had arranged to drive the guests back to their various abodes, and Gisela Mensch had announced over the telephone that she intended coming up that evening with her husband, so they could take their own family back with them.

After *Kaffee und Kuchen*, the actors scattered to gather together all they would need for "props." Madge had promised that, if they would take nothing from the salon, she would shut her eyes to anything else; and after Andreas had been coaxed to hang curtains across one end of the great room, and rig up a special lighting arrangement the salon was left severely alone by everyone. Some of them were busy in the den where Stacie still lay, printing programmes. Others were manufacturing dresses with pins and curtains, counterpanes, table-cloths, and sundry other articles.

At half-past eighteen, Nurse appeared, and Stacie was taken off to bed, despite her own protests that she wanted to see the fun.

"Stay up when you've been spending the last few days in your own room because you were so poorly? Certainly not!" said Nurse firmly. "To bed you go, and at once. If I let you stay up, you'll spend the rest of the week-end in bed, and I don't think you'll enjoy *that*!"

"It's hard lines, old thing," said Joey, who was with her at the time. "Still, I suppose Nurse is right. I'll tell you what; I'll slip up during the evening whenever I can, and tell you how things are going."

"Oh, no, you won't!" said Nurse. "Stacie is going to bed and to *sleep*. If you start playing games like that, she'll lie awake half the night, and be like a limp rag to-morrow. Say good-night to her, Jo, and let her go."

Jo said good-night properly, but when Nurse had rolled the chair along the hall to the lift, she relieved her feelings by pulling the most awful face she could conjure up after her, greatly to the horror of Violet Allison, who happened to come across the hall at that moment, and got the full benefit of it. Violet gave a squeak of terror, and scuttled back to the salon as fast as her legs could carry her, under the impression that Jo Bettany was going to have a fit, since she could think of no other reason for the violent squint she had suddenly developed.

Jo laughed rather shamefacedly, and pulled her face straight. She had not meant to frighten the little ones.

However, Violet had no chance to brood over it, for *Abendessen* was announced at that moment, and they had to hurry over it, so that the audience should not be kept waiting too long for the first of the tableaux.

The performance opened with a solo from Margia. This young person was destined by Herr Anserl to dazzle the audiences of two hemispheres. If he had had his own way, she would have given up her whole time to music. Luckily for her, the Staff saw things in a different light, and Margia had to take her full share of other subjects. She was to drop a good many of them and give the greater part of her time to her piano as soon as she was fifteen, but that was nearly a year away. She played, now, the minuet from Ravel's "Sonatine," and played it with a charm which delighted the audience. From behind the curtains, however, subdued giggles were to be heard at intervals, and once there was a thud, suggesting that someone had dropped a sledge-hammer on the floor. Margia went on with un-ruffled calm, and when she had finished, got up, dropped a grave little curtsey in response to the applause, and strolled out. Anne Seymour took her place at the piano, and the pretty old English nursery rhyme, "Boys and Girls, come out to Play," rang through the room. Anne was not gifted as Margia was; but she was clever at improvising, and she turned the quaint tune into a little dance, a march and, last of all, a song. The curtains were jerked apart, and the audience beheld a charming tableau.

It had been decided to give the Juniors their turn first, and then send them out to swell the audience. In this picture, five or six of them, including Violet, Greta, Bridget O'Ryan, and Emmie Linders, were standing in a broken circle. They wore short-waisted frocks which fell to their feet, and little caps, manufactured from handkerchiefs. The two end ones of the string held out their hands in welcome to those who were coming. The Robin made a charming little boy with long pantaloons, and a frill of goffered white paper round her neck. Laurenz Maïco of the black curls wore a yellow dress, and held a big bun in one hand. From a cleverly hidden step-ladder, which had been decked with greenery to represent a creeper-covered wall, Mary Shaw was to be seen climbing down. Little Gretchen Braun, who had begged permission to join the others for Half Term, was hanging over the top of the "wall," giving her a helping hand. The stage was darkened, but from another ladder in a corner Joey and Frieda held two electric torches each, to represent moonlight. The effect of the torches poked over the curtain hung up in front of this ladder was rather funny, but the audience overlooked it in the most obliging manner, and the Junior Middles got their full meed of applause. The finishing touch was added when Joey's golden voice rang out in the quaint old words:

"Boys and girls, come out to play!
The moon doth shine as bright as day.
Leave your supper, and leave your sleep,
And join your playfellows in the street.
Come with a whoop! Come with a call!
Come with a good will or not at all!
Up the ladder, and down the wall,
A halfpenny bun will serve us all!"

As Joey sang the last words, the curtains were pulled together again, and while Anne wove another little dance out of the old tune, they prepared the second picture.

This time, the little actors were in Dutch dress, and Biddy O'Ryan's long pigtails looked very well falling from under the pretty cap Simone had made out of two lace-edged dinner-mats and some picture-wire; while Kitty Burnett made a gallant Hans Brinker in huge, bepatched breeches. They carried Marie's biggest wooden bucket between them, and there was no need for anyone to call out the name of the rhyme. It was obviously Jack and Jill going up the hill!

For a minute the audience were allowed to gaze at the pretty picture. Then the curtains were closed again, and opened a few seconds later to show Jack on his nose, while Jill was balanced very unsteadily in a tumbling attitude. Just as the applause was ringing out, Jill suddenly lost her balance, and with a wild yell she pitched forward on to Jack, who uttered a compound sound—half gasp, half grunt—as her full weight landed on him. The next moment, he had grappled with her, and the pair were rolling over and over on the stage, locked in each other's arms. That was, naturally, the moment the curtains chose to stick. Elsie and Ilonka, who were in charge of them, pulled at them valiantly, but they got half-way, and then refused to budge. The audience was in fits of laughter, and all the wild tugging of the stage hands did nothing for the curtains. Finally, Joey strode on to the stage, grabbed Jill by her plaits, and Jack by a foot, and dragged them off, frowning so blackly all the time, that it put the finishing touch to the onlookers' hilarity, and they screamed as if they had never seen anything so funny before.

Once they were out of sight, Jack began to weep, and Jill to scold in a rich Kerry brogue; but Frieda managed to keep her head, and she hustled them both out of hearing. Elsie and Ilonka dragged the ladder forward and coaxed the curtains to behave themselves, and the stage was finally shut out from view. Anne began to play Edward German's "Shepherds' Dance" from the "Henry VIII Dances," and the third tableau was got ready.

This time, the curtains were pulled apart to disclose a dainty picture of Little Bo-peep, fast asleep beneath a haycock ingeniously arranged with a few bundles of newspapers, covered by a maize-coloured cloth that Madge seemed to recognise, though what it was, she could not think for a moment.

But she soon got it, and as the curtains were drawn together again, from the audience there arose a wild cry of: "My beautiful table-cover that Wanda sent me from Wien! How *did* those wretched children get hold of it? I've never dared to use it, it's so delicate. For goodness' sake, someone, fold it up carefully and bring it to me!"

The curtains parted, and Joey appeared. "That is *practically* all from the Junior Middles," she said, frowning severely at her sister. "They are coming to sit in the audience for the present, while we arrange the next tableau. Cornelia Flower will now sing 'The Skye Boat Song.' Everyone is asked to join in the chorus."

"Joey—Joey! Bring my table-cloth here!" implored Madge frantically. "I wouldn't have it marked for worlds, and you've got the edges trailing all over the floor!"

The announcer merely fixed her sister with a frigid stare, and vanished without vouchsafing a word in reply. However, as Gretchen Braun duly appeared with the precious cloth, her heart had evidently softened.

When the jubilant younger Middles had appeared in the audience, Cornelia came before the curtains, while Anne struck a chord. Corney had a sweet, clear voice, and though she could not hope to vie with Jo she sang very well for her age. The song was one that everyone knew, and they sent back the chorus with a will. The songstress certainly deserved the clapping she received, and she withdrew with a smirk of satisfaction on her face. Then Margia, who had come round to the front, changed places with Anne, and began to play the lovely "Menuet d'Exaudet," and the curtains, proceeding again by a series of jerks that made Madge wonder how on earth their supports would last out the evening if this were going on, parted to show a dainty scene.

Joey and Frieda occupied the centre of the stage, clad in full poudré costume. They had managed it by stealing the curtains from the nursery—as they were of cretonne, prettily sprigged with roses—and draping them round their waists over two of Madge's petticoats in a polonaise effect. Cotton wool—Jem had to lay in a fresh stock later on— made their wigs, and with patches manufactured out of sticking-plaster, fan for the lady and lace-edged handkerchief for the gentleman, they gave quite a good result. Behind them were two couples similarly attired, except that the rose-coloured curtains from the bedrooms had been utilised for their polonaises. It really was very pretty, and the audience were delighted with it. The curtains were closed, and an old harp which had belonged to Jem Russell's grandmother was brought forward. Then Frieda, still in her poudré attire, came forward, and the lovely folk-melodies of the Tirol rang through the room. She was received vociferously, and had to give an encore, which seemed to be just as well, judging by the sounds behind her.

First there was an agitated whisper of "Joey—Joey! Where are the green cloths?" which was answered by a hoarse "Behind you, *Dummgopf!*" in Joey's voice. Madge made a note to warn her young sister against using such rude epithets, but forgot it next moment as a crash resounded through the room, to be followed by: "Land of Goshen! There goes the ladder! I *told* you so!" easily recognisable as Evadne's contribution.

"What on earth are they doing?" whispered "Bill" to the hostess.

"I wish I knew," returned Madge sincerely. "I can only hope that we shall not find that part of the room in need of vital repairs before the night is over!"

However, at that moment the harpist ran her fingers over the strings in a final arpeggio, and when Frieda had vanished—presumably to help with the curtains—a magnificent scene was presented to the enthralled audience. Joey, nothing if not ambitious, had aimed at a representation of "The Golden Staircase." The "staircase" itself was made out of sundry boxes, a table, a stool, a chair, and two low step-ladders, along the tops of which rested a couple of broad planks on which were standing Vanna and Elsie, draped in their own sheets. Descending them, were Sophie Hamel, Evadne, Cornelia, Ilonka, Margia and Simone. The musical instruments of the original were represented by Sophie's violin, Rix's toy saxophone, a tambourine, two pan-lids (to represent the cymbals), and a harp made out of cardboard and string. The "stairs" were draped with green velvet draperies in which the horrified Madge recognised her two new portières, only just put up; and the balustrading on which the pair at the top were leaning consisted of a couple of scarves stretched across the embrasure of the french window and firmly nailed into place. The singing girls were Joey herself and Yvette Mercier. As for dresses, they had all robbed their beds, and Madge shuddered for the holes in her good linen sheets as she saw the light gleaming on multifarious safety-pins.

The audience clapped loudly, much to the delight of the actors, and Cornelia, already excited by the applause her song had received, forgot herself so far as to breathe heavily into her saxophone, which emitted a sound suggestive of a cat having its tail trodden upon. Jo forgot that she was in a tableau, and deliberately turned round to glare at the perpetrator of this outrage, which put the finishing touch to the mirth of the audience. Mercifully, the curtains were closed just then, and she had to go forward—still clad in her trailing draperies—to sing. She had chosen a very favourite song of the School's, and her golden notes rang out in Ernest Farrar's "Knight of Bethlehem." She was encored, of course. She came back, and gave them Ivor Novello's "A Page's Road Song."

When she retired, the curtains opened on Sir John Millais' picture, "The North-West Passage." Cyrilla Maurús was the girl, sitting at the feet of the old sea-captain, and in her pretty dress of pink art-muslin, with her long hair caught in a knot at the back of her head, an absorbed expression on her small, pointed face, she looked simply delightful. The old captain was a work of art. He was personated by Louise Redfield, the biggest girl in the School. Normally, Louise was a good-looking girl; but she had scraped her hair back from her face, and had provided herself with a beard made out of horsehair taken from the seat of one of the old-fashioned chairs that adorned Jem's surgery. They had also ransacked the doctor's wardrobe for trousers and a tweed jacket, while the collar had been made out of cardboard. The weather-beaten aspect of the face had been done with water-colour, and they had used up all Madge's vermilion and burnt umber. Unfortunately, Dr Jem was moved to murmur quite audibly that the old man looked as if he were in for a violent attack of scarlet fever! The result was a bad attack of giggles on the part of the "old salt," which was certainly not in keeping with his part. Cyrilla, too, was suspiciously pink, and might have been seen to bite her lips hard; but she managed to avoid the suppressed gurgles that issued from her "father."

After this, some of the Seniors came out and sang Vaughan Williams's setting of Christina Rossetti's poem, "Sleep." Meanwhile, Joey had called the Robin from the audience, rather to the surprise of the others. But the reason was forthcoming when the choristers had retired, and the curtains opened once more to disclose a most unexpected picture. Frieda Mensch, got up as an old woman, with frilled cap, shoulder shawl, and lines made with a soft lead-pencil, was standing over the little girl, who wore a pair of Jem's shorts, and an old blouse of Joey's. A chair had been placed in front of them, with a basin of soapy water and a cake of soap conspicuously displayed on it. The child's face looked as if she had been up the chimney, and Frieda, with a portentous scowl, was apparently scrubbing away at her.

" 'You Dirty Boy'!" shouted a chorus of delighted voices. "Oh, what a good one!"

Then the curtains closed again, and the audience were left to amuse themselves while the final tableaux were prepared. A great deal of hammering and chatter went on, and there were wild giggles every now and then, which were traceable to Vanna and Simone, two people rather addicted to giggling. But when at length the tableau was unveiled for them, the audience declared it was worth the long wait they had had.

Round the walls were tacked the green portières, and

fastened to them were the long sprays of wild roses which had been used the previous year at the Sale of Work. Perched on two tables, set side by side, were two William and Mary arm-chairs, the joys of Jem's heart, now draped with the bedroom curtains. In them sat a king—Vanna di Ricci—and a queen—Ilonka Barkocz. The king was glorious in a mantle made of the scarlet table-cloth from the kitchen, while his queen's robes were composed of the curtains which matched it. Their crowns were of cardboard, heavily gilt, with jewels of coloured papers gummed on. Steps had been made to lead to the thrones, and at the foot of them sat Evadne Lannis in page's costume long brown stockings and short tunic, provided by a jumper of Jo's. A fillet of green ribbon held back the thick curls that were always untidy, and she looked charming. Four tall footmen, attired in gym. knickers and coats with the linings turned outwards, stood at attention on either side. A lady-in-waiting, whose magnificent poudré gown later proved to have been manufactured out of two counterpanes and some lace dinner-mats, was standing with hand upraised to box the ears of a small page—this latter was Cornelia Flower—who was obviously flinching from the blow. A crowd of court ladies and gentlemen were placed in charming attitudes—and all quite plainly asleep. And over the whole hung the sprays of wild roses.

"Oh! The palace of the Sleeping Beauty!" cried the Robin, an inveterate reader of fairy-tales, from her place in the audience, whither she had gone after she had changed and washed her face. "Oh! *Isn't* it pretty!"

"But where is the princess?" demanded her bosom friend, small Laurenz Maïco.

"I expect she is in the tower-room, waiting for the prince," said the Robin seriously.

The curtains were jerked together by two of the footmen, who miraculously came to life to do it, greatly to the amusement of the audience, who guessed rightly that the girls had decided to include everyone in this tableau and its sequel, and had forgotten all about the curtains till the last moment. But it gave them time to arrange the finale during the shrieks of laughter that greeted the close of the first. Then the curtains parted for the last time, and showed the court awake. The king was sitting up with a most amazed expression on his face, and a hand on his magnificent beard of cotton-wool. The queen was settling her crown, which had been slightly awry in the last picture. The little page-boy at the foot of the throne had lifted his head from his arm and was staring at their Majesties with open mouth. The waiting-lady had her hand against the ear of the other page, whose face was screwed up in an expression which, as Dr Jack Maynard whispered, was more suggestive of his having overeaten himself than anything else. In fact, the whole court had awakened, and thrown off their briars. At the foot of the throne steps stood a magnificent couple. The parts of the Sleeping Beauty and Prince Charming had, with one accord been allotted to Jo and Frieda. As Anne Seymour had said, "Not one of us has hair like Frieda's. When it's spread all over her shoulders, it'll look like a mantle of gold—just the thing for the Sleeping Beauty. And Jo makes a topping boy!"—which had settled the matter at once.

Jo, clad in a green velvet bridge-coat for which her sister had been looking most of the afternoon, her own dark-green dancing-knickers, with lace ruffles at throat and wrists, and one of Jem's fencing foils girt about her waist by the Robin's best gold-silk sash, made a dashing and gallant prince. But Frieda bore away the palm. She was arrayed in robes of golden silk which Madge recognised with a gasp of horror as being the new curtains for the drawing-room—they had never even been put up yet! They were girdled by a zone of deep blue knitting-silk, and her sleeves, which hung nearly to the hem of her gown, were also of blue—this time, the two beautiful coverlets which had been sent by Frieda's parents for Baby David's cot at the time of his christening. The resourceful girls had turned them inside out to show the blue lining, for the actual coverlets were of marvellous, hand-made lace; and Madge's face when she discovered the use to which they had been put was a study. The veil was Mrs Russell's own wedding veil, which Joey had unearthed and it was caught over her flowing locks by a cluster of briar roses at either side. Frieda was a pretty girl, even if she could never hope to rival lovely Marie von Eschenau, and in this guise, with her hair falling to her hips in long, fair curls, she was a perfect picture.

An outburst of applause that outdid everything the audience had hitherto accomplished greeted the tableau;

and then Dr Jem made a leap for the piano, and proceeded to thump out with one finger the air of the Bridal March from "Lohengrin" amidst the protests of the actors and the auditors. In the middle of all this, the poor curtains were jerked at once more. The much-tried supports gave way, and they fell with a melancholy "flop!" just in time to let the audience see the slapped page-boy turn and wrestle with the lady-in-waiting; and the prince stumble over his foil which had caught between his legs, and grab at the princess to save himself. The princess, in her turn, grabbed with equal futility at the leg of one of the chairs used for the thrones, and it promptly tilted off, while the queen, with a frantic yell, plunged heavily among the court ladies and gentlemen who echoed her shrieks.

Of course no one was hurt—not even the chair, which was the first thing Dr Jem rushed to examine. Then he turned his attention to the girls, and finding that there wasn't even a bruise to doctor, gave it as his opinion that the "sweet little cherub that sits up aloft" to keep an eye on the sailors has an easy time compared with the one who has schoolgirls on his hands. And then Nemesis descended in the shape of Madge!

"Where on earth did you find my portières?" she demanded. "And those table-cloths?—Frieda Mensch, do you mean to tell me your sleeves are made of the coverlets your people gave Davy? Take them off, for pity's sake, and be careful with them. I value them more than I can say!—And, Joey, I'll thank you to give me my bridge-coat. I might well hunt in vain for it this afternoon! And who gave you permission to get my veil?"

"And the clean curtains for the windows—and the counterpanes, Madame!" wailed Marie who had just discovered them. "It will be necessary that they are ironed again, so crumpled are they!"

"Do you *mind*?" asked Jo, with remarkable sangfroid.

"Mind?" began her sister indignantly. Then she stopped and began to laugh. "Well, as it's only for once, perhaps not. Your tableaux were charming, girls—we've all enjoyed them immensely. But do go and put on your proper frocks now. There is a feast for you in the Speisesaal before you have half-an-hour's dancing."

"Cheers!" cried Jo the irrepressible. "Come along, you people! Let's get changed at once!"

With cries of delight, they raced off to get into their frocks; and then ten minutes sufficed to clear up most of the mess before they went to the Speisesaal, where they sat down to a feast of chicken sandwiches, jellies, trifle and cakes from Innsbruck. When, finally, they dispersed for the night, it was with the firm conviction that this was going to prove the very best Half Term they had ever had.

## CHAPTER XIII

## A GLORIOUS TIME

SUNDAY passed peacefully. When they awoke, they found that the storm had risen, and there was no question of their going out. Even church had to be given up. A lull in the blizzard occurred at ten o'clock, and Dr Jem took advantage of it to fling on his cap and coat, and go off to the Sanatorium. But ten minutes later the snow was coming down harder than ever, and until he had rung up from Captain Humphries' office at the Sanatorium, his wife was restless and anxious.

"If this goes on, I shall be stuck here for the day," he told her over the telephone. "Also, the wires will be down. I've rung them up at Spärtz to warn them, so that if nothing gets through after sixteen o'clock this afternoon, they'll know why, and send someone up to see to it as soon as possible. How are the babes getting on?"

"Do you mean David and the twins? They are quite happy in the nursery."

"And the elder babes?"

"In the salon. *They* are rather worried about not getting to church. I'm going to give them books, and suggest that they should sit and read quietly for an hour as there can be no service. Did you call in at the hotel?"

"Yes. They are storm-bound, too, but quite happy. Ring up the Annexe and Gisela when we've finished. Gottfried has gone back to 'Das Pferd' now. That old sinner is getting on all right, by the way—under the impression that he's going to die, of course, but he'll soon be past that."

"I suppose it's as well. I'll ring up the others. And Jem!"

"Well—what?"

"You are not to attempt to get back unless the storm is much less severe than it is now. Promise me, or I shan't have a moment's peace until I see you again."

"Very well, dear. Don't worry. I won't come unless this blizzard lifts considerably. Take care of yourself."

"Of course; I always do!" And with this, Madge rang off, and then called the Annexe and her friend Gisela Mensch. Being reassured of the well-being of all, she left the telephone, and went to the salon, where the girls were gathered round the great stove that warmed the rooms almost to summer heat. She saw gloom on Elsie Carr's face, and went to her first.

"Elsie, dear," she said, "I'm so sorry you can't go to Lilias to-day as we arranged. But if it clears up to-morrow, you can have *Kaffee* with her."

"That's very decent of you and Dr Jem, Madame," said Elsie, the gloom clearing a little.

"Girls!" She turned to the rest. "We can't get to church. This weather makes it impossible. But don't you think we had better read a little for an hour? I have several saints' Lives, and the Bible in both the Revised and the Douay version, as well as 'The Imitation of Christ,' and one or two other books of the kind. If you will come with me to my bedroom, you can each choose one, and then you could read down here till half-past eleven or so."

"I'll come, for one," said Joey, getting to her feet after she had gently put the Robin off her knee.

"I also," added Simone.

"And I"—"And I"—"Me, too," came in quick succession from the others.

Madge smiled, and led the way to her pretty bedroom, where one of the two white bookcases was filled with books on religious subjects. The girls chose what they wanted, and then went off to the salon, where they sat about in various nooks and corners, reading quietly to themselves. Even the Robin snuggled up to Joey with her catechism, and when she knew the questions she had to learn, the elder girl heard them for her.

Half-past eleven brought Stacie downstairs in her chair. Nurse had not been able to get along to "Die Rosen," but Madge was able to lift the child out of bed, and dress her in her loose clothes, all specially made to give her as little trouble as possible. Then it was only a question of rolling her chair along to the lift and bringing her down into the hall, whence she could be wheeled into the salon.

She received a joyous welcome, and, demanding an account of the proceedings the night before, laughed over some of the happenings till the tears stood in her eyes. After that, they talked quietly about their Sale of Work for the next term, and the free wards where stood the beds they themselves had given. After *Mittagessen* everyone rested, and then Madge brought a book, and read to them. The evening was filled in with making jigsaw puzzles and reading, and finally they went to bed after what Margia Stevens, as a little girl, had described as "such a *gentle* Sunday."

"It looks cheerful for to-morrow," said Elsie, as she surveyed the dizzy dance of the snow from her bedroom window that night.

"It may clear up," said Evadne hopefully. "You never know."

"And if it does," said Simone, who had come to their room to borrow some tooth-paste, as her own had given out and Joey had very little left, "let us beg Madame to permit that we build a fort and have a snow-fight as we did last year."

"That's a great idea!" exclaimed Evadne. "Bully for you, Simone!"

"Topping fun!" agreed Elsie. "The Annexe folk could join in, too."

"Join in what?" demanded Jo, who came along at that moment to demand whether Simone meant to spend the rest of the night there.

"Why, a snow-fight," said Evadne.

"Jolly! Oh, Mad-*ame* will agree like fun!"

"If only it isn't snowing to-morrow," sighed Elsie.

"It mayn't be," said optimistic Jo. "I don't see how it can go on like this much longer! We'll be buried alive if it does, and have to shove a flag or something up the chimney like those people in that gorgeous book by John Oxenham."

"Which book is that?" demanded Elsie.

"*Their High Adventure.* It's in the Senior library, and as you're a senior now, you can get it. Ask Sophie for it on Wednesday."

"I will. It sounds topping."

"Bags me it after you!" cried Evadne.

"Why aren't you people in bed?" demanded a fresh voice from the doorway, and Madge was among them.

"We were planning a snow-fight for tomorrow," explained Jo.

"Oh, yes, Madame! And the Annexe to join in too!" added Simone eagerly.

"If the snow has stopped, I don't see why you shouldn't. In fact, it's a very good idea. But do you people know that it's nearly half-past twenty-two? And though it *is* Half Term, I don't think you ought to be any later. Trot off to bed, and no more talking, remember."

"Yes, Madame," said obedient Simone. "Come, Joey.— Bonne nuit, Madame."

"Bonne nuit," said Madge with a smile. "Remember, girls! no more talking."

They retired to bed with all speed, and were soon fast asleep. Even Jo, who was renowned for her early waking, slept on till seven in the morning; and as for Ilonka, she had to be shaken awake! But when they were finally roused, they all sped to the windows and pulled back the curtains to look out. Cries of joy greeted the sight that met their eyes. The snow had ceased some time before, and the whole landscape, as far as they could see, was shrouded in a white garment so dazzling, that Madge issued orders to the effect that no one was to go out unless she first put on coloured glasses.

"We don't want any cases of snow-blindness," she said firmly, before she went away to ring up the Annexe, the hotel, and "Das Pferd" to explain the arrangements for the day.

It seemed to the excited girls that *Frühstück* would never come to an end. Dr Jem had managed to get back home late last night, and he made matters worse by starting an argument on some trivial matter and insisting on having it carried to its logical end. The people at "Die Rosen" could hear shouts outside which warned them that the others were arriving; but the tiresome doctor held on his way till Joey put an end to it by jumping up and dashing to the window. "Oh, *bother* you!" she cried. "Every solitary soul is waiting there for us, and you go on arguing about nothing!—Madame, mayn't we go?"

"Yes; off with you!" said Madge, having mercy on them, for she thought they had been kept long enough in suspense. "Remember what I said about snow-glasses, and mind you all wrap up. I'll come along in a moment and review you all."

"Mind you put on climbing-boots," called the doctor after them as they raced from the salon.

"What about the twins?" asked Jo, coming back for a moment.

"They are far too little to be turned out into the sort of hurly-burly you people will make. They, and some of the tinies from the Annexe, can have their own fight in the back garden. Don't let them come with you."

"We don't want them," retorted Jo. "Too much responsibility. Shall I go and tell Rosa to wrap them up and send them down to the back garden?"

"Yes, please. And tell her to be sure that they have on snow-glasses."

"Right-ho!" And Jo galloped off to the nursery, where she bade Rosa make her charges ready, and answered Rix's importunities to come with her by a hasty "No, Rix! You and Peggy and some of the others are to have your own fun by yourselves in the back garden!"

Then she dashed off to her own room without paying any heed to Rix's plaintive "Wants to come wif *you*, Auntie Joey!"

"Simone, you're ready, aren't you?" said Joey, as she struggled madly with her nail-protected boots. "Run and get Rufus; there's a dear!"

Simone went off, and presently a fearful clatter on the stairs proclaimed that the others were coming down pell-mell.

"They can change in the cloak-room when they come in again," said Madge to her husband. "Think of those boots on my beautiful old oak!" Then she went to greet the rest, having wrapped herself up in a great shawl and donned the snow-glasses on which she had insisted.

People who have never seen the Alps under winter conditions have no idea of the dazzling whiteness of the snow under the winter sun. Many people are unable to stand the glare with unprotected eyes, and suffer from that unpleasant complaint, snow-blindness, when everything seems to swim in a red light. Years before, when the Chaletians had been new to this sort of thing, they had been badly afflicted, and they were careful not to run any such risks now, for the complaint is most disagreeable, even if it is only temporary. So even the babies from the Annexe wore their tinted glasses, and there were shrieks of laughter at the appearance of everyone in "goggles."

"Well, how do we arrange things?" demanded Grizel Cochrane.

"Miss Carrick and I will pick sides," suggested Miss Wilson who had been chatting with her ex-Head. "—Of course we're joining in!" as a chorus rose around them. "Do you think you're going to have all the fun to yourselves? Miss Stewart will back up Miss Carrick, and I'll take Miss Cochrane. The rest of you—all but Robin Humphries, Peggy Burnett, Inga Eriksen, Laurenz Maïco, Gredel Hamel, Margaret Browne, and Cecile le Brun— will be on one side or the other. You small folk are to go to the back garden, where you will have your own snow-fight with Miss Leslie, and Peggy and Rix Bettany will join you. When you are tired, you can all ask Madame if you can help to get something ready for us to eat. We shall need it by that time, I imagine!"

She sent a laughing glance across to Madge, for this was a part that they had arranged over the telephone. Both knew that "the babies" would be very grieved and indignant at being sent off by themselves. But some of them were too young and some too frail for it to be possible to let them be exposed to the rough and tumble of the older girls. But giving them the task of preparing food for the elders would flatter their sense of importance and wipe away their disappointment. And so it turned out.

So Mrs Russell swept off the smaller party, accompanied by Gisela Mensch, who had brought her small daughter with her, and was going to run up to the nursery with her and leave her in the charge of the competent Rosa and Miss Leslie, who had offered to be responsible for the small fry.

Meantime, the Seniors and Middles clustered round the four mistresses, who picked sides as quickly as possible and then separated. Juliet had claimed Joey, Frieda, and Simone, Miss Wilson out of mercy leaving the French girl with her adored Jo. "Bill," herself, had Vanna, Bianca, and the whole of the Quintette. The rest were sorted out carefully, and the fight began.

A little ring of bushes formed a natural fort, and the holders of it—Juliet's party—were given ten minutes to fortify it and strengthen the walls. The rest made ammunition for the whole party; though once the fight began, it would be a case of everyone for herself. When the ten minutes were up, Miss Wilson called Juliet, and they stood together talking at an equal distance from both sides. Then they suddenly parted, and each dashed back to her own army, crying "To battle!"

Led by Grizel, a small file of girls began to steal round the back of the fort while "Bill" and the main body charged heavily on the front. Miss Stewart and Juliet held the chief posts there; Joey, Frieda, Simone, and four small Middles from the Chalet having been told off to watch the rear while the rest spread themselves round the sides and the front.

The first casualty was Biddy O'Ryan, who received a mouthful of snow, and was rescued, spluttering wild things in her native brogue, just as Anne Seymour leaned out from the fort to drag her in. Once inside, she would be a prisoner, and so out of the game altogether. At the same moment, Grizel and her band of bravoes reached the point for which they were making, and hurled themselves on the rear of the fort with wild yells that would have turned a Comanche Indian green with envy.

Crash! Louise Redfield, leaning over a bush to grab at Cornelia Flower, overbalanced and tumbled out among the enemy, who shrieked delightedly, and dashed to grab her. But Louise was quick, and she was on her feet and climbing madly back to safety before they could reach her. She left a long strip of her shawl on one of the bushes, but she was not a prisoner.

Wild screeches from the front told them that something was happening there, and Grizel, feeling her post to be where she at present was, sent off a French child, Mélanie de Vos, to scout. Mélanie had come to the Annexe that term, a very good, shy little girl. But she was that no longer as she came tearing back to announce that Violet Allison from the Chalet had been captured from the holders of the fort, and had had her face well scrubbed with snow.

Nor was she the only victim. More than one girl was captured by either party; and the climax came when Miss Wilson, severe and grave Science mistress at the Chalet, had tripped over a long "sucker" from one of the bushes, and been caught by Jo, who, not recognising her—or so

116

she vowed—stuffed a handful of snow down her neck as an additional insult to a fallen foe. "Bill" was a sport, however, and she merely made for Joey when she had regained her feet, and returned the insult with interest!

It was glorious fun. The snow was dry and powdery, and no one was badly hurt, though there were a few knocks and bruises sustained. The worst casualty was Ilonka Barkocz, who was kicked on the shoulder by accident. But it was no more than a nasty knock. Still, Miss Wilson sent her in to keep Stacie Benson company at the salon window. By this time, the little ones had come in too, and were buzzing round feeling their importance at getting coffee, and sandwiches, and cakes ready for "the big girls" when they should come in.

Rix had distinguished himself by tripping over a hidden tree-stump, and crashing on to a stone, whence he had emerged with a bumped forehead on which a lump as big as a pigeon's egg was fast developing, while there were distinct signs of a black eye adding to his beauty. Boy-like, he soon pulled himself together. As his Uncle Jem said when he attended to the wounded warrior, he was a plucky little chap, and he would have considered himself disgraced if he had cried before "zose girls." Indeed, it was Peggy who made the fuss, and she was indignantly pushed away by her brother, who declared that he didn't want to be "messed over!"

The fight lasted more than an hour, and then Madge rang the bell loudly, and summoned them all into the house. "Into the cloak-room, all of you!" she cried. "Change your shoes, and then Jo will show half of you to the west bathroom, and Simone will take the others to the one in the south wing.—All members of Staff go to my bedroom—Robin will take you. Any damages to make good?"

But there were none. Grizel, with a queer feeling as she remembered the snow-fight of the days when she had been head-girl at the Chalet School, lifted her hand to her head where a small white scar remained to remind her of a feud which had nearly had a bitter ending for more than one of them.

"I wish Deira had been here," she said to Juliet as they followed the rest of the Staff, piloted by the Robin, to Mrs Russell's pretty bedroom. "I should like the chance of another snow-fight with her."

"I wish she were here myself," said Juliet, with a quick glance at her. "All the same, Griselda, you shouldn't think of it. Past things are past. Madame wouldn't like it if she knew."

"I owe Deira a debt for a lesson in keeping a rein on my tongue," said Grizel. "If I hadn't spoken as I did, she'd never have lost her temper as she did, and that would never have happened. The mark doesn't show a bit, either," she added inconsequently.

It was not long before they were all swarming into the salon, and then the small folk were in their element, handing coffee and sandwiches and cakes.

"I don't feel as if I could eat any *Mittagessen*," said Ruth Wynyard sadly as she eyed the last bite of her fourth cake.

"Guess *I* can't—I'm as full as I can hold," was Cornelia's inelegant way of putting it.

"There isn't going to be any *Mittagessen*," said Jo, who happened to be near, and who passed over Cornelia's rude remark for the sake of the holiday. "When we've all had as much as we can eat, and are rested, we are going to walk to the other end of the alm, so that those who haven't been up here before can see as much as possible of it."

"Bully!" sighed Cornelia.

"I'll tell the world we're having one glorious time!" was Evadne's method of summing up the state of affairs as she got up to get her third cup of tea.

CHAPTER XIV

A LITTLE SCIENCE

At fourteen o'clock by Continental time, they set off, led by Joey and her beloved Rufus. It was a wonderful walk, for the clean, crisp air acted like a stimulant on them, and the scenery was beautiful.

Down at the foot of the mountain lay the lake, coated with thin ice which turned it black in its rim of white snow. The villages and hamlets scattered about its shores had the appearance of toys dropped by the hands of giants. Round them rose the mountains, grander than ever in their winter garb with only the blackness of the pine forest on their lower slopes to contrast with the purity of the snow. Above, the sky lay grey and wintery, for the pale November sunshine of the morning had vanished shortly after midday, and the girls had no need of snow-glasses now.

And it was the same the whole way along the alm. Wonderful views opened out to them; and in the south, they could see the Zillerthal Alps, white beneath their crown of snow. They got back to their various domiciles by sixteen o'clock, and had *Kaffee und Kuchen* before they all met at "Die Rosen" for dancing and games. That was the real end of the Half Term, for the next day saw the Chalet people climbing into the coaches to be taken down to Briesau; while the Robin trotted back to the Annexe after a sorrowful farewell to her beloved Jo.

It must be admitted that at first the girls seemed to settle down very well after their happy holiday. Even Thekla came back much better. At least she and the rest of her form did not quarrel quite so much as they had done in the earlier part of the term. Cornelia, with the hope before her of attaining the Lower Fifth, worked hard, and was unusually steady. As for the Sixth, no less was expected of them. Simone, with the prospect of the Sorbonne before her in the following autumn, could always be relied on to do well at her work. She was a clever girl, and delighted in all her subjects. It would never do for her to go back to Paris and do so badly that people who had been at French schools should be able to say this was because she had been at one run on English lines. In some ways, she had a pull over them, for she could speak English, German, and Italian with fluency, and knew a fair amount about the literature of the four countries whose languages she had studied. But in other subjects, she knew well that the more strenuous work of French schools might have advanced girls of her own age beyond her. But at least it should not happen if she could help it.

As for Frieda, Carla, and Vanna, they contrived to get through their work with a very fair amount of success. Sophie Hamel was the daughter of a clever man who was very ambitious for all his children, and she did her best not to disappoint him. The rest worked steadily for one reason or another, all except Joey Bettany.

Jo was a problem. Mathematics she loathed, though when she chose to give her mind to them, she could do them as well as the majority. Drawing she hated with a deadly hatred, and all drawing lessons had been a series of pitched battles between herself and Herr Laubach. In music, again, she was little use at any instrument, though her sister insisted that she should continue with the piano. Her voice, on the other hand, was a wonderful gift, and she revelled in her lessons with "Plato." Languages and their literature came to her easily, but sewing was her bugbear. Years of training had made a fair needlewoman of her, but none of the Europeans considered her work as anything but poor.

It was on the Tuesday following Half Term that things began to happen. The Fifth, in the two divisions of which four of the Quintette had been pitchforked, was invariably a problem with which to reckon; and so was the Fourth. In these two forms were most of the mischievous girls of the School.

That morning began with Elsie Carr upsetting her coffee over the table. It was an accident, so Frieda, who was at the head of the table, said nothing when the younger girl had apologised. Ilonka Barkocz could generally be relied on to follow Elsie's example. The pair had a quiet, unemotional friendship, and Elsie, as the stronger character, led Ilonka very much as she chose in all ways but one—of which more later. Evadne, Margia, and Cornelia were a different proposition. The other two were well over fifteen. These three were still fourteen, irresponsible, and did what they could to liven the School on all occasions.

On this occasion, Evadne and Cornelia, who were seated at opposite sides of the table, began a game of "kick your opposite," which Evadne herself had originated in her early days. It consisted in trying to kick your opposite number so gently that only she knew of it, and it was difficult enough, for anyone caught at it was sent from the table at once. This morning, Cornelia began it. She kept her eye on Frieda, waited till the prefect was engaged in pouring out fresh coffee for Giovanna Rincini, and then made a long leg and kicked Evadne so suddenly that that young lady, who happened to be drinking at the time, choked violently.

"Evvy, what, then, is wrong?" demanded Frieda in the German which was the official language for Tuesdays.

"I—I choked," said Evadne with a very red face. "My coffee—er—went down the wrong way."

"You must be more careful," said the prefect.

Across the table, Evadne scowled at the triumphant Cornelia who was sitting with a bland smile on her face. "Wait till I catch you!" she muttered under her breath.

"You can't—they're under my chair," retorted Cornelia, referring to her legs.

Evadne was not going to be put off in this fashion. She cast a cautious eye at Frieda; decided that the elder girl was too busy to notice her; and slid down on her seat till she could stretch, when she kicked, hard and sharp. A gasp and a violent jump from Lilli van Huysen on Cornelia's right hand informed her that she had missed her mark, even while Frieda looked up and said firmly, "Evvy, sit up at once, or leave the table."

Evadne wriggled back, casting a look at Cornelia that made that young lady gurgle. As her mouth was full, it was her turn to choke, and Frieda, without guessing the actual cause, was astute enough to know that there was something unlawful going on. She kept a keen eye on her table for the rest of the meal, and they behaved properly, for Frieda, though slow to rouse, was a tartar, once she was really awakened.

But if Evadne and Cornelia thought they were going to get off so lightly, they were mistaken. As they were going out of the room, Miss Wilson touched them lightly. "When you two have finished your cubicles, come to the Staff Room," she said quietly; and then let them pass on.

That was all, but it was enough. Once they were outside, the guilty pair faced each other, dismay clearly written on their faces.

"Crumbs!" said Evadne gloomily

"Bill saw!" exclaimed Cornelia. "Oh, my hat!"

"Cornelia, you've been told not to use that expression," observed Jo, as she passed them. "Pay your fine, please!"

"Can't—I haven't any money till Saturday, as you jolly well know," returned Cornelia defiantly.

"Then I'll tell Matron to dock it off your pocket-money on Saturday. And don't be impertinent, please, or you'll get a bad mark as well," returned Jo, who had wakened up with a nagging toothache and was not in the sweetest of tempers in consequence.

Having already received *one* bad mark, and fully

expecting another, Cornelia shut her lips tightly at that, but her state of mind was not improved by the rebuke. She followed Evadne upstairs, seething with rage, and made her bed with a vim that nearly sent the bedding through to the floor. However, she was not given to sulking, and having worked off her temper that way, she was comparatively calm when she joined Evadne in the corridor outside. They descended the stairs in the prescribed silence, and walked along to the Staff Room, where they found Miss Wilson busily correcting the Third Form Nature Study, and not improved thereby. She looked up as they came in and frowned "what were you two doing at *Frühstück*?" she demanded.

"I—er—kicked Evvy under the table when she was drinking and made her choke," admitted Cornelia, who, whatever her faults, was truthful enough.

"And you, Evadne?"

"I—tried to return it," said Evadne uncomfortably.

"I see." The mistress glared at them. "And so you two, big girls of fourteen—wait—aren't you nearly fifteen, Evadne?"

"Ye-es," said Evadne.

"Quite so. Then you two behaved like two small children from Le Petit Chalet—and at mealtime, of all times! *All* bad manners are disgusting; but bad table-manners are, perhaps, the worst."

Silence; but judging by their squirming, she had got home. She waited to see if they had anything to say; then she went on: "Did Frieda know what you were doing?"

"She—she told us—to sit up or—leave the table," confessed Evadne with cheeks rivalling the scarlet woolly the mistress was wearing.

"I see. Did she know what you were doing?"

"No-o-o-o."

"Very well, then. You can both take your meals at punishment table for the rest of the day. And if you have to be spoken to again for this sort of thing, I shall ask Mademoiselle to let you sit at Staff table with us. You may go now."

They went; but if dismay had been on their faces when she had first summoned them, there was desperation there now. The punishment table was not instituted for people of their age, but for Juniors who were untidy eaters. It was a little table, standing by itself, and everyone knew

122

why girls were sent there. To go to it, even for one day, was a disgrace from which they felt they could never recover. Her final threat of the Staff table had quenched them completely. Also, they had not liked what she had said about bad table-manners. It was a very subdued pair therefore that went down the passage to the form-rooms.

On the way, they met Lilli van Huysen, who stopped them. "Evvy, why did you kick me so?" she demanded. "I was not harming you at all, and you made me jump and splash my clean jumper with my coffee. I wish you would not behave so! It is like great, clumsy boys!"

"Oh, dry up!" flashed Evadne. "It wasn't meant for you, anyhow.—Guess Corney Flower's the meanest girl alive!"

Now when you have tried to take as much of the blame for an unpleasant episode on your shoulders as possible, it is annoying to be called mean into the bargain. Cornelia had a hot temper, and she flared up at once. "Mean yourself, Evvy Lannis!" she retorted. "Guess you're a real cry-baby! You can't take the least mite of a joke!"

"Yes, I can!" snapped Evadne. "But it was all *your* fault! You started it, and you ought to be real ashamed of yourself!"

"Well, I'm not! I'm not a mite ashamed! So there, you rubber-necked, left-footed *glumph*!"

This was tempting Providence with a vengeance.

Cornelia had the usual luck of people who do such a foolish thing, for Miss Stewart, coming along to the Fifth Form rooms, reached them just as she spoke, and got the full beauty of this gem of Americanese.

"Cornelia!" she exclaimed in horrified tones.

Cornelia, thus brought up short, went redder than she had done before Miss Wilson, and said nothing. Miss Stewart proceeded to tell her what she thought of such expressions in crisp, trenchant English, and then went on her way, leaving Cornelia dazedly realising that she had to pay a treble fine to the fine-box; and that she had been awarded two bad marks, which meant that when the rest were dancing happily on Saturday night, she would be in Matron's room, hemming a sheet. If Joey Bettany detested sewing, Cornelia regarded it with a hatred besides which Jo's faded to nothingness. Not all her years in a school which boasted of the good needlewomen it turned out could make her otherwise than a bad worker, and she knew that there would be a battle over that sheet before she had finished with it. Even Evadne's resentment vanished before this calamity, and she slipped a new pencil into the hand of her late foe with a whispered, "Keep it!" as some kind of solace. Cornelia was too much depressed to do anything but accept it mechanically before she turned in at the door of her own form-room, while Evadne went on to hers.

Evadne whispered to some of the others what had occurred, and this contretemps helped to settle the Fifth for the time being. This was just as well, for their form-mistress, Miss Stewart, came in just after Evadne, and she was peppery, though it made no difference to her popularity with the girls. She was looking displeased about something; her pretty lips were set in a straight line, and there was a frown between her brows. They had no desire to rouse her temper, so Register was got through very smoothly, and they went in to Prayers as properly as they could in consequence.

But if the Fifth were prepared to behave themselves, it was more than the Fourth were. They had begun the day by growling at the weather. Since they had come down from the Sonnalpe, they had been kept indoors by the swirling snow-blizzards, and they hated it. Monday had found them restless and fretting to get out; Tuesday finished it. Even drill and gym during the day and country and morris dancing at night could not take off the edge of their energy, and, as Miss Wilson said later on, they were like so many little engines, stoked up to top-notch, and on the verge of an explosion.

During Prayers, the reverential atmosphere kept them all quiet; but once they were back in their own room, the Fourth boiled over.

As it happened, their first lesson was with little Mademoiselle Lachenais who was famed for being invariably amiable. She kept order, it is true; but nobody had ever seen her out of temper. This morning was to break *that* record.

It began with *dictée*, in which the girls kept complaining that they had not caught what was said. Mademoiselle Lachenais repeated the phrases, at first with a smile; later on, the smile vanished. However, they got through it at last, and she told Cornelia to collect the papers, and prepared for conversation. To-day, she beamingly informed them that they would discuss *"L'hiver."*

The rule in these lessons was that each girl must say at least three sentences which should be in grammatical and idiomatic French. Also, they must not repeat one another. They enjoyed this as a rule, for it was free speech to a great extent, and it was quite usual for the form to chatter steadily through the three-quarters of an hour allowed for it. It was excellent training for them, and they learned to speak French fluently and colloquially.

To-day, there was silence after the subject was announced, and Mademoiselle had to call on someone before she got anything. Finally, "Cyrilla, est-ce-que tu aimes l'hiver?" she demanded.

"Non! Je l'haïs!" declared Cyrilla bluntly.

Mademoiselle looked surprised, as well she might. The girls usually loved the cold weather here, where winter sports were provided for them and there was any amount of skating, tobogganing, and ski-ing. Besides, this was not what she called "conversation." She tried with Greta Macdonald, and fared no better—and it says much for the feeling in the form, for Greta was a shy, quiet person, who was generally as good as gold. It is true she did not exactly repeat what Cyrilla had said, for she remarked, "Je déteste l'hiver!" But even so much from her was something at which to wonder.

Mademoiselle Lachenais persevered. She got nothing better. One after another the Fourth declared their detestation of winter, and they came to a deadlock. Mademoiselle looked silently at the twenty-four naughty girls who made up the form, and her lips set in a hard line. "You will sit there until you have something more to say to me," she said in a voice that made them all jump.

They saw that she meant what she said, and all began to rack their brains for something more. The something would not come, however, and when the bell sounded for the next lesson, they had been silent for nearly fifteen minutes. Mademoiselle gathered together her books, an unusual flush of colour in her cheeks, and fires burning in her eyes. "No one will have any Break," she remarked before she left them. "Nor will there be any free time for you until I have heard at least ten original sentences from each one of you about *L'hiver*. And if you have not spoken them by the end of *Abendessen* this evening, I will give you each five order-marks, and requests that you remain in bed all day *dimanche*."

With this dire threat she left them. As Miss Leslie, who was responsible for all mathematics in the School, and who had been waiting at the door, came to them at once, they had no chance of talking it over, and Miss Leslie gave them no peace. Throughout that lesson she worked them hard, and not a girl had two minutes in which to get together her scattered thoughts and manufacture the ten sentences Mademoiselle had demanded.

Break brought them no respite. Mademoiselle came to them almost at once, followed by Sophie Hamel, the prefect on Break duty, who bore their milk and biscuits on a tray. She set it down, and Mademoiselle Lachenais dispensed them herself. She bade them all finish as quickly as possible, and sipped her own cocoa while they swallowed the milk. When it was down, she collected the mugs at once, and then they set to work. Sorry work it was, too. Cornelia managed to stammer out something about water freezing in winter, and added that the wind was cold. Ruth Wynyard, a jolly, tomboyish person, said briefly that they had snow-fights in winter, and Christmas came then. This gave several people a cue, and for the rest of Break they manufactured sentences on *"Noël,'* until Mademoiselle pulled them up.

"There is more of winter than Christmas time," she reminded them. "I wish to hear of other times, also. This is not a conversation on Christmas."

A Russian child, Olga Petrovska, mentioned the New Year, and spoke of the tales of New Year festivities she had heard from her parents. Finally, Cyrilla Maurús contrived to finish her punishment with a description of the Carnival held every year on the Tiern See. She, Cornelia, Olga, and a little Breton girl, Jeanne le Cadoulec, had finished when the bell rang again for lessons, and they were sent off to the geography room where, for once, they welcomed Miss Wilson and all her works, and managed to get a little rest. It was not until the gong had sounded for *Abendessen* that the last four, Ruth Wynyard, Enid Sothern, Alixe von Elsen, and Klara Melnarti, were set at liberty. Still, their hard work kept them from worse mischief, much to the relief of the Staff, who had their hands full long before then with the malcontents of the Fifth, who, having recovered from their various quenchings when the afternoon came, really *did* cause an explosion, and gave the School a fright it long remembered.

Tuesday afternoon at the Chalet was the afternoon when the two Fifths had their two hours in practical chemistry. They marched down to the "Chemmy Lab." after their midday rest and were greeted by Miss Wilson who had some pieces of crystalline substance ready for them. They sat down at their benches, and proceeded to spread out their paraphernalia—test-tubes, crucibles, and beakers. Each girl had a bunsen burner to herself, and these had been lighted. Then "Bill" informed them that they were to find out the nature of the substance, using the tests she had told them at the last theoretical lesson.

"Test it with acid to see if it gives off a gas," she said. "Try it with litmus paper, and make notes of what you discover. See if it is soluble, and if so, with what. You had it all last Wednesday, so you have plenty to do.— And, Evadne! *Tasting* does *not* come within the tests for it. Remember, please! You aren't a baby now, you know."

Evadne, who had slowly been coming to boiling-point whenever she remembered the indignity of eating *Mittagessen* at punishment table now reached it. She dared not say anything, but she vowed inwardly that she would show "Bill" something! Miss Wilson, not heeding the scowl with which her remark had been greeted, went across to Rosa van Buren and began to assist her. The rest applied themselves more or less to their work.

Elsie Carr worked steadily, making notes as she had been told, and going through the various tests suggested with great conscientiousness. She was fond of science, and had lately made up her mind to go to the Royal Holloway College and read for her degree if she could. Margia Stevens did not take the subject, and was spending these two hours in piano practice, which fact rejoiced the heart of gruff old Herr Anserl, who had vowed that Margia would be, if not in the first rank of concert performers, at least very near it. This term, she had dropped science, art, and most of her mathematics for extra music. The only other girl in the form who did not take science, was Thekla, who had never done any before she came to School. Thus, there were twenty-one girls in the class, and Miss Wilson had been heard to declare that she sometimes wished there was only one! Two of the twenty-one were Evadne and Ilonka, the latter of whom hated science, and

127

was always begging to be allowed to drop it; and these two stormy petrels were almost enough for one person in a laboratory.

Evadne looked about her after a very feeble attempt at dissolving her specimen in distilled water. Everyone seemed to be working hard, and Miss Wilson herself was busy, explaining something to Yvette Mercier who was not exactly brilliant. This was too boring for words! Evadne decided that she must liven things up a little.

With this amiable object in view, she got off her seat and brought a little of the sulphuric acid prepared for them. But in getting it, she also helped herself to a jar of some blackish-grey powder that happened to be standing on a bench not in use. It had been left there by Carla von Flügen that morning, when the Sixth had their two hours of practical work. After it was all over, Carla admitted that she could not remember clearing her bench, as she had been called off in a hurry by Matron, who had noticed in Break that she seemed to be husky, and wanted her for gargling.

Removing her crucible from the bunsen burner, Evadne cautiously tipped a little of the powder on to the crystalline substance. Then she added the sulphuric acid, and set the vessel back, turning up the burner to full strength. She had had the sense to remove both the acid and the powder-jar to a safe distance before she did so, and it was as well. Otherwise, this story might have had a melancholy ending. As it was, there was trouble enough.

The mixture fulfilled the young American's wildest hopes, for almost as she turned up the burner, there was a prolonged "his-s-s-s!" and the whole contraption went up in an explosion that resounded through the building, even reaching faintly to Le Petit Chalet; while fumes of the most noxious description filled the room. Over all were to be heard Evadne's shrieks, and the girls, tearing pell-mell from the laboratory, were brought up short.

Then Miss Wilson sprang to the rescue, caught up a blackened object, and bore her away, followed by her terrified pupils, while the swirling snowflakes came dancing in at the broken windows—not a pane of glass in the room remained intact—and began to cover up the soot on Evadne's ruined bench, while an awful smell stole through the entire room. Elsie Carr sprang back, and after a hasty look round to see that nothing was burning, slammed the door to after her, and then raced along to the gas meter to turn off the gas. As for the other forms, they were under the impression that the Chalet had been struck by a thunderbolt at the very least, and came pouring out into the corridors.

It was an exciting time. "Bill" carried Evadne up to the Sanatorium where Matron at once took charge of her, and began to peel off the rags that were all that remained of her clothes. Mademoiselle sent for the two men who worked on the place to come and see that the laboratory was really in no danger of burning, she herself ushered the girls through the kitchens to the farthest outhouse where they would be in comparative safety; though it was unlikely, in view of the terrific blizzard that was raging, that anything could take fire. Finally, when Evadne had been washed—she was as black as a crow—bandaged and laid between the sheets, with Matron sitting beside her to see that she slept off the effect of the shock, and the rest had calmed down a little, it was possible for the Science mistress to find out what had happened. She had feared that the laboratory would be completely wrecked; but luckily, beyond the broken windows, the bench at which the experimenter had been working, and the clothes of that lady herself, no great damage had been done. Evadne herself had escaped marvellously. What she had used, they did not find out till Miss Wilson had had time to take an inventory; and even then, they could never be sure, as the concussion, besides breaking the windows, had shattered several jars near at hand, and their contents were in a mixed confusion on the floor. But that it was something of an explosive nature—especially when doctored by Evvy—seemed fairly certain. She had been soot from head to foot, and the curly hair round her face was badly singed, and so were her garments. But she had instinctively flung up an arm to shield her face, so that beyond a long scorch from elbow to wrist, she was uninjured. She had been working at the far end of the room by herself so no one but herself was hurt. By means of opening doors and windows they got the smell out of the house in time, and the shutters were fastened across the laboratory windows to stop the snow from coming in.

"Altogether we have come off more lightly than I dared to hope," said "Bill" next morning as she looked pensively round at the mess in her usually spotless laboratory.

"Evadne has learned a lesson *this* time—she won't play any more pranks in here; that's certain! And it was the bench that someone spilled hydrochloric acid over last term. It might have been worse!"

"I have almost decided to stop these lessons for Evadne," declared poor Mademoiselle Lepâttre who had passed a bad night as a result of the shock. "That child might have been killed—to say nothing of the others!"

"Not she!" said Miss Stewart with conviction. "She's like a cat—got nine lives, and always falls on her feet!"

"Oh, I can't do without Evadne," laughed Miss Wilson. "She ought to do well when she's got a little more sense. And till then, I must just keep a firm eye on her. In any case, part of the blame is Carla's. The Sixth know they must not leave anything about. If that stuff—whatever it was had been locked up, the chances are that nothing would have happened."

So it was left. But Mademoiselle took good care that Evadne should know why she was permitted to continue her science lessons, and Evadne was grateful. She always grumbled at them, but she admitted to her own bosom friends that they helped to relieve the monotony at times.

"They certainly do when you start experimenting," remarked Margia to whom this had been said. "But the next time you want to manufacture an explosion, Evvy, for goodness' sake choose something that will explode with a smell that does *not* remind one of rotten eggs!"

The prefects had plenty to say on the subject; but since one of their own body had been partly to blame for it, they were not quite so scathing as they might have been. The worst comment came from Thekla. *She* screwed up her nose, and said, "That is what comes of teaching *girls* the same lessons as *boys*! Their brains are not wise enough to reason as those of boys do, and so one has such an event as this!"

However, as this general remark hit at everyone, she was severely snubbed by all, and Evadne relievedly turned to the subject of the Staff Evening, which was the next excitement, knowing very well that her own kind would soon forget her doings for that.

## CHAPTER XV

## STAFF EVENING

AFTER all, Cornelia was excused that hated sewing. In view of all that had happened, Mademoiselle agreed that the punishment might be cancelled. Evadne's exploits had given everyone such a shock, that it was some time before the Middles were anything but amazingly good. As for Corney herself, she was so much upset by what had happened, that she went about like a ghost for the next few days. Accordingly, when Evadne came downstairs again, looking white and subdued, she found the School lying under a spell of peace.

"There's one thing—it can't last long," said Joey Bettany the next evening, as she got her books together. "Otherwise, I should imagine our babes were qualifying for a speedy translation to a better world!"

"The Staff Evening comes next Saturday," said Frieda. "That will wake them up a little. And you must admit that we have been able to do our work properly, even when we have had to take prep."

"And that's something that I'll bet has never happened before in this School," said Jo. "What's more, I feel pretty sure it will never happen again."

"There goes the bell!" sighed Simone, who was on prep duty that night. "Well, at least I shall be able to do my essay and my maths."

Saturday found everybody in a state of high excitement. The function known as the Staff Evening was to fall on St Andrew's Eve this year—it had been arranged as a Hallowe'en party but had had to be postponed. The girls were going to try all sorts of ideas, and had planned some experiments which they thought it would be as well to leave till the Middles and Juniors had gone off to bed.

Their consternation when Mademoiselle announced at *Frühstück* that she was going to permit everyone to sit up till ten o'clock, as it was Staff Evening, may be better imagined than described.

"What on earth are we to do about it?" demanded Joey of her clan, once they were safely away from the rest.

"We must make a new programme!" gasped Simone.

"We have no time for that," said Frieda. "Guides will come, and then walk, since today it is not snowing, and this afternoon we must decorate. So how can be rearrange the programme?

This was no more than the truth, and the girls looked at each other gloomily. Finally, Marie von Eschenau nodded her pretty head sagely. "We must use the one we have, and make the best of it," she said.

There was nothing else to do. So, hoping that the Staff would understand and that they would take it all as fun, the girls went forward with their preparations. *Kaffee und Kuchen* took place at sixteen o'clock promptly, and after it was over, the Sixth turned the rest out of the Common Room, and proceeded to set various tables ready. Fritz brought in a huge wooden tub, and then carried buckets of water which he emptied into it. Simone and Marie disappeared, and returned laden with baskets full of apples. Joey brought a huge bag of chestnuts; and Frieda filled the baskets from the dining-room tables with nuts of all kinds. A chunk of lead and an old iron spoon lay on one of the broad window-sills, and a bucket of water stood near. A wooden box was filled with candles, and Anne Seymour and Louise Redfield put up a weird-looking contraption in one corner.

Finally, mirrors were brought downstairs, and one of the big trestle-tables they set up for Hobbies Evenings was placed at one end of the room, and covered with a big blue cloth. On this, the girls put jellies, creams, sandwiches, little cakes, and, in the very centre, a cake which measured thirty inches in diameter, and seemed to be heavily covered with white icing. Adorning it, were horseshoes, wishbones, new moons, and crossed keys. A smart pink sash was tied round it, and finished off with the most imposing bow that Simone's French fingers could concoct. When this pièce de résistance was in place, the girls heaved a sigh of relief, and then went flying off upstairs to change, for time was hurrying on, and the "evening" was supposed to begin at eighteen sharp.

They had put at the bottom of their invitations, "Please come in clothes that don't matter," so they themselves proceeded to don the shabbiest garments they possessed. Then they caught up their bath towels, and ran downstairs, ready to play their part as hostesses.

By eighteen, the guests were beginning to arrive. The first to come were Miss Stewart and Miss Wilson, always tremendous friends, and always doing things together. They were warmly welcomed, and then Paula von Rothenfels took charge of them, and led them to seats by the stove where a glorious fire burned. The two most popular people in the School were followed by Miss Leslie, Mademoiselle Lachenais, and two "outside" people, Miss Sarah Denny, who taught Italian and Junior music, and her brother, Mr Denny, better known to the School as "Plato" who was its Singing master.

After that, the visitors poured in, and the hostesses were kept busy in receiving and entertaining them. The babies from Le Petit Chalet came over in charge of their own mistresses, Miss Norman and Miss Edwards, while Miss Durrant, the Head of Le Petit Chalet, made a dignified entrance with Mademoiselle Lepâttre. At last, everyone had come, and then Anne and Joey went to the piano to open the entertainment.

Joey had elected to sing "Sigh No More, Ladies!" by Aiken, and Anne played the pretty, rippling accompaniment very charmingly. "Plato" listened to his most promising pupil with his head on one side, and Jo watched him anxiously. His profession was his life, and if she made any mistakes, she knew quite well that he would never think twice of telling her of them, and turning the affair into an impromptu singing lesson. However, she got through without any trouble, and then went thankfully to sit down beside Miss Wilson, while four of the Sixth played a movement from one of Brahms' Quartettes for violin, viola, 'cello, and flute. It went very well, and after it was over, Simone recited one of Victor Hugo's poems. Finally, the whole Sixth sang Schubert's setting of "The Lord Is My Shepherd," and Charles Wood's lovely arrangement for "Music, When Soft Voices Die." That finished the musical part of the entertainment, and there was a little rustle of expectancy as Joey, as head-girl, went to the table to seek sandwiches. Luise came in with the big coffee urn and Fritz followed with a huge jug of milk for the babies. The Sixth waited on their guests very prettily, and everyone enjoyed the little supper. Even Evadne began to look more like herself, greatly to the relief of Mademoiselle and Matron, who had been quite worried about her.

"What are you people planning to do with us, Jo?" asked Miss Leslie. "I hope it's nothing very outrageous? I see you have towels here, so I suppose we have to duck for apples. But what else are you going to do for us?"

"Can't tell you now. You'll see later." And Jo escaped with her cakes before any more awkward questions could be asked.

When at length everyone had had sufficient, Marie rang the bell, and Luise and her satellites came to carry the remains away. Only the big cake was left, and, to the amazement of the visitors, that had not been cut so far. Now they saw why.

"We are going to have this first," said Jo grinning. "Then if any of you feel that you want to wring our necks, you'll look at this, and forgive us.—Mademoiselle, would you please come here?"

Mademoiselle Lepâttre got up and went to the table. Then the guests understood. The "cake" was not a cake at all. It was a round, wooden box, covered with white, embossed paper, and got up to look like a cake. Joey had lifted the top off, and requested Mademoiselle to accept a blue ribbon. The Head took it, and, at a word from her niece, Simone, pulled it. A parcel came out, and she returned to her seat after thanking the girls heartily, while Miss Annersley took her place, and pulled at a yellow ribbon. There were parcels for everyone, even the babies, and what that wonderful "cake" had held, it would take pages to tell. Mademoiselle found in hers a dainty handkerchief edged with pillow-lace. Miss Annersley had a scent sachet, as she was known to love lavender. "Bill" and "Charlie" each got a collar of point lace. Everything had been made by the girls themselves, and everything was charming. The little ones had dolls, jigsaw puzzles in bags, and sets of dolls' furniture, also in bags.

Finally, the cake was emptied, and then the fun of the evening began.

Jo dropped some apples into the tub, and blandly invited the Staff to come and bob. Mademoiselle Lepâttre cried off, but Miss Annersley proved game for it. She took the towel handed to her by Simone, and draped it

134

round her neck. Then she knelt down, and began to chase an apple round the tub, the rest standing round, and showering advice and comments at her.

"Try for that big chap, Miss Annersley!" suggested Jo, pointing to a mammoth specimen. "He oughtn't to be too bad to catch."

Miss Annersley paid no heed to her. Selecting a small one, she pushed it with her chin to one side of the tub, and then, with a swift, downward movement, got her teeth in it, and rose with it in her mouth amidst cheers from the girls.

"Bill" was not so lucky, and she had to go down to the bottom of the tub before she got the monster pointed out by Jo. But she finally rose with it and retired to the stove, where she set to work to rub her head vigorously.

But meanwhile, Marie had been doling out chestnuts, and some people strayed away from the tub to put theirs on the shovel, first naming one for themselves, and the other for a friend. Then came the fun of watching to see if they jumped apart, or burnt away, or cooked steadily. Simone the superstitious gave a cry of dismay when the nut she had named for Jo suddenly hopped off the shovel into the red heart of the fire; while Cornelia, seeing the one she had christened for herself flame up unexpectedly, remarked, "So that's what'll happen to me! It ought to have been Evvy."

This took up some time, for everyone was anxious to get an apple, as well as try her luck with the nuts. Meanwhile, Jo had set a cauldron on a small stove set at the farther side of the room, and broken up the lead in it. The heat soon melted the lead, and then she called the guests, six at a time, to come and try their fortune.

"What do we do?" asked Ilonka Barkocz.

"Take this ladle," said Marie, putting it into her hand. "Now lift a little of the lead in it, and drop it into this cold water. The shape the lead makes will tell your future."

Ilonka solemnly did as she was told, and a queer, distorted shape was the result.

"I think myself it's a coffin," said Jo, knitting her brows.

"Nonsense, Joey! It is a train, and Lonny is going to travel!" replied Frieda sharply.

"I think it is a torpedo," said Margia Stevens pensively.

"There must be going to be another war, and Lonny will be on a ship that's torpedoed."

"What pleasant prophecies!" laughed Miss Annersley, who had come up behind them. "Now *I* think it's a chest, which probably means that Lonny will become wealthy sooner or later."

"Will you have next shot, Miss Annersley?" asked Anne.

Miss Annersley shook her head. "No; some of you other people try first.—Thekla, let us see what the future holds for you."

Thekla drew back. She rather despised all this. However, the atmosphere of the School was doing its duty, and she was already a nicer girl than the one who had come in September, so she took the ladle, dipped up her lead, and dropped it into the cold water, where it assumed the unmistakable form of a circle.

"That's a ring!" cried Marie. "You must be going to wed soon, Thekla."

"Not just yet, I hope," laughed Miss Annersley. "You are rather too young for that, Thekla. Who is next?"

There were several people to come next. Indeed, everyone wanted to try this game, and the lead held out only by a miracle. The evening was well advanced by the time everyone had had a turn, and the girls were anxious to go on to something else. This was the time for Louise's arrangement. She called ten people to her, among them Miss Nalder and Miss Wilson, and while Joey coaxed some others to try their luck with ears of corn, Louise carefully set "Bill" opposite a large apple which hung at one end of a flat cross-piece of wood, and invited her to try to catch the apple in her mouth.

"Is this a new form of 'bobbing'?" laughed "Bill."

She made a dive at the apple. It swung away, and the other end of the cross-piece came round, and slapped her lightly on the cheek. It had been padded, so did not hurt. The girls all tittered loudly, and Miss Wilson herself laughed. "Bad shot!" she said lightly. "May I have another, Louise?"

"Two more," said Louise, choking surprisingly.

The apple had come to rest again, so "Bill" made another dart at it. This time, she tried to get it from the other side, and again she set the board swinging, and again the padded end struck her, this time, on the other cheek. The titters grew louder, and "Bill" felt puzzled. She took her third try, and managed to get her bite this time.

Then "Bill" stood aside, and Louise called for Cornelia, who was still examining her piece of lead. "Corney, come and try this kind of bobbing."

Corney came. She opened her big eyes very widely at the sight of the mistress, and smothered a giggle. Then she took her place, and opening her mouth widely, tried to make a bite. In vain; the board swung round, and caught her on the forehead. "Bill" began to smile sympathetically. Then she suddenly gasped as she saw the child's face.

"Where's a mirror?" she demanded.

Elsie produced one, and Miss Wilson beheld herself with amused horror. The padded end of the board had been blackened, and every time it had hit her, it had left a large smudge on her face.

"You little wretches!" she exclaimed. "No wonder you all giggled! I *thought* it was rather more than was necessary for seeing me miss the apple. How many more people are you going to take in with it?"

"As many as we can catch," replied Louise swiftly. "You don't mind, do you, Miss Wilson?"

"Not in the least," said Miss Wilson lightly. "But I'd better wash my face if you want to try it on anyone else."

"We've towel and sponge over here," said Elsie.

"Bill" sponged her face, and they parted to let her go on to try her luck with the ears of corn. This was Joey's arrangement. A big basket of ears had been brought into the room, and set on a table. One by one the people who wanted to consult the oracle were blindfolded, and led up to the basket. Then they had to pull out the first ear that came to hand. Joey explained that a tasselled ear foretold great joy; a short one, a gift; while a red or yellow one meant no luck at all.

Mademoiselle Lepâttre was persuaded to try this, and drew one of the largest ears in the basket.

"Good luck for you!" cried Jo. "What a whacker!"

"My turn, now," laughed Miss Annersley. She let Joey blindfold her, and then drew quickly.

"Oh!" cried Marie. "That is yellow, and so means no luck at all!"

Miss Annersley smiled. "I don't mind, Marie dear. I may have luck with something else. Now who comes?"

Most of them tried it, and it was only stopped when Evadne was discovered eating her ear of corn.

"Raw grain at this time of night!" cried Miss Nalder in horror. "I think it will be just as well if Matron has her medicine ready."

"Evvy!" exclaimed Miss Wilson. "What *will* you try to eat next?"

Evadne reddened. She had a perfect craze, surprising in a girl of her age, for tasting everything—hence the warning she had been given in the laboratory at the time of the explosion. The others had teased her about it, and the Staff had not been behindhand, either; but she was incorrigible.

By this time, the apple and pad had palled, so everyone was round the fire. Now came Marie's turn. She produced twelve candlesticks of the flat variety each with a candle set in it. These she arranged from one end of the room to the other in two lines a good distance apart.

"And what is this, mon enfant?" asked Mademoiselle.

"This is to see which months will be fortunate for you," said Marie. "Each in turn must jump over the candles. Those that remain lighted will be happy months; but those that go out will be months of bad luck. Now who will begin?"

"Well, what about yourself?" suggested Jo.

"Oh, but won't Mademoiselle try?"

Mademoiselle shook her head and laughed. "You forget, chérie, that I am an old lady now, and not so agile as I once was. But Miss Nalder—"

"Oh, I don't mind beginning," cried Miss Nalder. "Light them, Marie, and we'll see what luck I have."

Marie lit them, and Miss Nalder, beginning at November, leaped lightly over them, one after the other. Up one side, and down the other she went; and when she had reached the last, the twelve little flames were still burning brightly.

"What a jolly year I must be going to have!" she said, laughing, as she returned to her seat.

The girls applauded her effort heartily. Later, they wondered at it. The Junior Staff were prevailed on to try this, and big Miss Durrant did it as well as the light little Gym mistress. Miss Norman put out three lights, and

Miss Edwards seven. Then Mademoiselle Lachenais was called upon.

Now Mademoiselle Lachenais was small and dainty, and the girls expected to see her go the round as easily as Miss Nalder. But they counted without their host. Mademoiselle shut her eyes, leaped as high as she could, and landed on both feet with a thud that shook the room. The tiny light flickered and went out promptly. With an agonised expression on her face, the foreign languages mistress repeated her tactics on the second. It was blotted out, too. On she went, the girls not daring to laugh, and suffering severely from keeping their laughter in. When the final thud came in a dead silence, Mademoiselle Lachenais looked back, and saw that not a single candle remained alight. She threw up her hands with a shriek of horror. "Ah! Mais c'est affreux! What bad luck lies before me!"

She looked so really scared, that Marie hastened to comfort her. "It is only a game, Mademoiselle. See; some-one else will do it—Jo?"

"Rather!" said Jo promptly. "Light them, Marie."

Marie lit them, and Jo set off. She got over the first three in grand style. Then she misjudged her distance, and leaped not over, but *on* to the fourth, which came down with a sizzle and a smash that made a fine mess of grease, especially as the candlestick upset, and Jo sat down abruptly, her long legs shooting out in front, and sending the candle before her flying into the sixth, which collided with the wall, and went out in a flurry.

"Three at one stroke!" gasped Frieda, who was nearly weeping with laughter. "Oh, *Joey*!"

Joey got up, looking slightly crestfallen. "I never expected that to happen," she said dazedly.

"Come and try these others," said Marie, choking back her laughter as well as she could.

Jo went, and contrived to finish the round without dis-gracing herself any further. Then she retired, to be well teased by Miss Annersley and Miss Wilson, while Frieda herself hopped neatly over the whole twelve—Marie had brought another to take the place of the squashed one.

The girls found this fine fun, though the Junior Staff, with horrified eyes on the clock, insisted on marshalling their little band, and taking them off to their own house. The Sixth went to see them off, and came back just in time to see Thekla taking her place. Throughout the evening, Thekla had seemed to be enjoying herself. It is true she had begun badly, for she had had an argument with Matron over the dress she should wear. The domestic tyrant had caught Miss Thekla just about to put on a blue muslin frock over her frilliest underthings, and had promptly ordered her to remove them and get back into the sensible gym-knickers they were all to wear. She had refused to listen to a word, and had only gone when she had seen Thekla beginning to remove them. But Thekla was obstinate. Once Matron had gone, she had refastened her petticoat. She dare not do anything but put on her brown velvet frock, which was the ordinary wear of the girls in the evenings; but she argued that no one was likely to ask her what she was wearing underneath.

Thus, while the girls who were sensibly clothed came to no harm, it was a different matter when she began to leap, wearing a petticoat of muslin, made very full and frilly. Just as she was leaping over the third candle, it suddenly flared up, and the flame caught the edge of one of the frills. The petticoat was too long for the velvet frock, and Thekla had tucked it up in a tape tied round her waist. But the exercise had loosened the tape, and the frills slipped down. At once the inflammable muslin was ablaze, and Thekla, screaming at the top of her voice, was rushing wildly to the door with some idea of making for a bathroom. It was not allowed, of course. Miss Wilson and Miss Stewart were on her in a moment, and threw her on the ground, while they beat out the flames with their hands. Joey, with a wild desire to be helpful, seized the big tub of water in which they had been ducking for apples, and flung its contents over the group on the floor. Water, apples, and a towel which had been dropped in by accident and left there, showered on the luckless trio, while Jo herself, staggering under the weight of tub and water, slipped, and crashed down on top of them, soaking herself as thoroughly as they were soaked. Any fire left about Thekla gave up the ghost after that. Mademoiselle rushed to the spot, ejaculating and exclaiming, while Miss Nalder pulled Jo to her feet, assisted by Mr Denny, who had watched the whole proceeding with amazed eyes. His sister snatched up two of the other towels flung down, and began to scrub at Jo's drenched frock, while Matron, without a word, went flying upstairs to see to hot baths and blankets and call to Luise from the kitchen to set on a jorum of milk to heat.

This ended the evening. It was obviously impossible to go on when four of the company were streaming with water and several of the others not much better. There was a small pond on the floor, and in the bustle and scurry, baskets of nuts and apples, as well as chairs, had been upset. Those of the guests who lived out of the School got ready, and departed. The wet ones were sent off to bed, where Matron dosed them with quinine and cinnamon, and big drinks of treacle-posset. The rest set the Common Room to rights—as well as they could for giggling when they remembered the faces of Miss Stewart and Miss Wilson as that icy douche of water mingled with apples and a towel had descended on them.

As for Thekla, beyond a slight scorch on one leg, she was not hurt, though she was upset by the shock of the accident and her unexpected shower-bath. Matron got her between the blankets as quickly as possible, and, for once, did *not* improve the occasion; though she made up for that two days later when the young Prussian was feeling almost herself again.

The one to come off worst was Jo. She was kept in bed all next day, for she had had a serious illness the previous year, and they were still inclined to be anxious about her on occasion. Thus, she missed a very special walk which had been planned since Half Term. Also, Miss Wilson, the Guide Captain, gave her a severe talking-to for losing her head as she had done.

"How you *could* be so silly, Jo, I can't think," she said. "You've been told over and over again what to do in case of fire. You've got your First Aid badge, too; but I must say I think you've got it under false pretences if that's all you can do when a fire really happens. You might have dropped that heavy tub on someone, and hurt them badly— to say nothing of the risk of giving someone pneumonia by drenching us with icy water at the end of November! I am very disappointed in you."

Jo was sadly crestfallen. Indeed, when she was allowed to join the others she seemed so depressed that they let her down very lightly.

But one good thing came out of it all. Thekla was so much impressed by the way the Guiders had flung themselves on her, beating out the fire without thought for themselves, that she declared that she meant to ask permission of her parents to join the Guides as soon as she possibly could. And when Sophie Hamel came to ask how she was, she answered her as pleasantly as possible.

"It strikes me," said Jo later on, when she had cheered up and was her usual insouciant self again, "that it needs *accidents* and *shocks* to reform people. Look at Stacie! She used to be a regular little nuisance; and since she ran away and got hurt, she's quite changed. And now this is making Thekla almost human. After another term or two here, I shouldn't wonder if she didn't turn out to be quite a decent sort!"

"Well, it does not seem to have changed *you* very much!" said Marie with a chuckle. "You have had many shocks—and given us many, too—but you are not much changed, Joey!"

"Ah," said Jo with a calm satisfaction that left them all breathless. "But then, you see, *I* was so nice to begin with!"

## CHAPTER XVI

## THE CHRISTMAS PLAY

When the people at the Annexe heard the accounts of Evadne's accident and the Staff Evening, Juliet and Grizel first sighed for the dear old days when they had been just happy-go-lucky schoolgirls with the rest; and then Juliet suddenly became the Head.

"That settles it!" she said decidedly. "I shall tell Madame that the girls can't learn science up here. I wouldn't have *that* responsibility for anything!"

"We haven't got Evvy, my dear," Grizel reminded her.

"Evvy's not the only one. I know that so far our girls haven't shown any signs of the particular madness that appears to be the main characteristic of that crew, but that's not to say that they mayn't develop it. No, thank you, Grizel, I have as much on my shoulders as I care for at present. No science here so long as *I* am in charge!"

"And that mayn't be for long," said her friend, referring to her engagement.

Juliet coloured furiously. "You know quite well that Donal and I can't be married for three years at least. I hope I shall be here till then. I want to be married from here."

"Do! And I'll be your bridesmaid."

"No; only Joey and the Robin will do that. But you shall be in attendance, Grizel," she added. "Anyway, it's three years ahead, and you may be married yourself by that time."

"No jolly fear! I mean to be like Joey and live a bachelor woman!" retorted Grizel firmly.

"I don't think Joey will end up like that," said Juliet thoughtfully.

"She always vows she will. However, there's time enough for that. At present, we've got to arrange for this emigration."

Every year, the girls at the Chalet School had given a Christmas play at the end of the Christmas term. Mrs Russell always wrote them, fitting her parts to her people, and they were always highly successful. The dress rehearsal was attended by the people round the lake and the domestic staff. Then, on the last day before the end of term, all those parents who could manage it came up to the Chalet, and the play was given as perfectly as possible. There was no charge made for admittance, but a collection was taken before the play began, and the results went towards making Christmas happy for any children at the Sanatorium. The little plays were very simple, but all the more beautiful for that. The girls were trained to take their parts with the utmost reverence, and the entire Staff threw themselves heart and soul into the business of training them. In the Tirol and the countries bordering it, the people are fond of pastoral and miracle plays, and the Chaletians had seen a great many. Their high-water mark was the great Passion Play of Oberammergau, to which they had been taken the summer before; and their own production meant more to them than ever this year.

It would have been hard to exclude the Annexe people, even if they had not been required. The Robin, with her childish beauty, was always in demand; and there were one or two others who ran her close when it came to choosing cherubim, baby angels, and so on. Therefore, the elders had put their heads together and decided that the pupils at the Annexe were to migrate to the Chalet and Le Petit Chalet for the last fortnight of term, so that they might have their share in the School play.

The great blizzard which had ushered in the winter was over. The crisp, pure air would suit the people from the Sonnalpe at present; and all that remained to be done was to make arrangements for the transport of the Annexe pupils and Staff.

There were many meetings at "Die Rosen" for it was not easily settled. Even the new coach road at the other end of the alm seemed likely to prove a risky business for coaches.

"It isn't only a question of ourselves," said Juliet on the last occasion. "There are all the school-books to take down, for I suppose they'll do *some* lessons? And then there's all the luggage. No one will be coming back here till next term."

"What about the Robin and me?" demanded Grizel. "*We're* not going to London!"—with a grin which made Juliet blush.—"We are all coming up for Christmas. And are the twins and Stacie coming down with us?"

Madge shook her head. "Certainly not the twins! I wouldn't dream of loading that responsibility on to anyone else's shoulders. Rix gets naughtier every day, and Peggy is just a little slave to him. And I scarcely think Stacie will be fit for it, either."

"Certainly not," said Dr Russell. "She is much better; but she's not fit for all that excitement. No, Grizel. The twins and Stacie must remain up here; and you and Robin ought not to need much down there. I propose that you have your things sent straight over here."

"Well, that will save a lot of trouble," said Grizel. "And how *are* we going to get down, please?"

"By sledge," said Gottfried Mensch. "We've engaged four big sledges with mules to draw them, and you'll go down the coach road to Wiesing, and take the train from there to Spärtz. Other sledges and mules will meet you there and take you up the Maurach road."

"And what about getting back?"

"You'll come back the same way. Only there won't be so many of you, of course. We're rather lucky this Christmas. Except for the English and American girls, everyone is going home. The rest are off to Kufstein for the holidays, so we shall be clear of them," said Dr Jem cheerfully.

"Then I think we ought to be getting back," said Juliet, rising. "There is any amount to do, and only tomorrow to do it in. Ready, Griselda?"

"Rather!—Oh, don't bother to come, Dr Jem! It's a beautiful night, and no one is likely to run away with us."

"If they did, they'd drop you at the first light," said Dr Maynard with a grin.

"How rude!" Grizel elevated her nose.

"But how true!" chuckled Dr Jem. "You had her that time, Jack!"

Grizel stalked out of the room with dignity, and Juliet followed her after anxiously assuring Dr Jack Maynard that it was all pretence on Grizel's part.

"As if I didn't know it," he laughed. "Don't worry, Juliet. I understand Grizel. She and Joey are going to have the holidays of their lives this Christmas!"

"If you are going to torment them all the time—" began Juliet, and paused before concluding, "—well, I shouldn't advise it. Jo can be awful when she begins!"

She left after that, and for the next two days life was very full for everyone at the Annexe. Saturday morning of that week saw them all flying over the snow-covered road in big sledges drawn by mules whose bells made merry music on the crisp, frosty air. It was not a very long journey to Wiesing, the little town at which the Kufstein-Innsbruck express stopped for just long enough to enable them all to get in; and then they were whirled away to Spärtz, where they were met on the platform by no less a person than Herr Anserl. He had nothing but love for the Robin, and he picked her up and hugged her fondly before he condescended to notice anyone else. Then, with her still in his arms, he explained his presence there. The previous day he had been up at the Chalet for music lessons as usual, and had heard from Mademoiselle Lepâttre all about the coming of the Annexe to the Chalet. He had, accordingly, made all arrangements to meet them, and here he was!

"And, in the Speisesaal at my home, there awaits you a little feast," he said. "You will lead the way, Fräulein Juliet."

Juliet stood in too great awe of the gruff old "Vater

Bär" to do anything but obey him. She led the way and they were soon in the long, narrow Speisesaal of his quaint old house. There the great, jade-green porcelain stove made the atmosphere summer-warm, and Herr Anserl's old house-keeper presided over a table laden with plates of *Kuchen* and *Torten*, and a huge urn of hot, milky coffee. They were all feasted. Finally, they were all packed in, and set off for the lake. After the somewhat break-neck journey down from the Sonnalpe, the road up to the Tiernsee seemed quite tame. Finally, they were on level ground once more, and going round the head of the lake in grand style.

Around the shore they dashed till they reached Seespitz, where they had to leave the sledges as the road to Briesau was too narrow for them. Some of the mules were hastily unhitched and laden with baggage; the rest were tied to the fence running round the *Gasthaus*. Then they set off. Of course it should have been a proper "crocodile," but Juliet and her Staff were merciful, and did not insist on it. So the Robin ran on ahead with Amy Stevens and Renée Lecoutier, Simone's little sister; and the rest followed them, the "old" girls being careful to see that the newcomers did not stray. It was not long before they reached the low fence that cuts off Briesau peninsula from the rest of the lake-shore; and from there to the high barrier of stakes and withies which surrounded the School grounds took them a very few minutes. The Robin swung back the gate, and raced up the path to the door at top-speed, Renée and Amy after her. At the same moment, the door opened, and Joey, wrapped in a huge shawl, appeared on the step. The Robin gave a little cry, and fell into the elder girl's open arms sobbing with excitement and happiness. Margia and Simone came running at the head-girl's warning cry, and grabbed their small sisters. Then Mademoiselle Lepâttre appeared, with the rest of the School flocking round her, and for a few moments it was difficult to make out anything, for everyone talked at once and there were at least six languages going.

Finally, Joey turned, with her arm still round the Robin. "Three cheers!" she shouted. "The *whole* of the Chalet School is here now! Oh, what a time we shall have!"

The cheers were given with a will; and then they all went indoors, for *Kaffee und Kuchen* awaited them, and even the gorgeous meal they had had with Herr Anserl was forgotten now. The fresh, chilly air had put a keen edge on the most fanciful appetite.

The evening was one of excitement, for everyone had so much to discuss. Sunday was a quiet day, spent as they always spent it. But with Monday came the first of the rehearsals, and the fortnight that followed went down in the annals of the School as "that *topping* time we had before the play."

It was not that they had not given other plays before, but this was quite a different affair from all others. For one thing, Mrs Russell had decided to give them a Pageant this year, and they had a noble time getting it ready. In the mornings they had lessons as usual. The Annexe Staff helped there, as well as with the dresses, which work occupied most of their spare time. The twenty-two girls who went to make up the Annexe were drafted off to the various forms, and most of them soon found that working with small numbers and working with twenty other girls, or even more, were two very different things. As for those who had been sent to the Annexe from the School, they were so thrilled at finding themselves back amongst their old surroundings, that they quite lost their heads, and the prefects complained that prep was no longer a time of peace.

But if the mornings and early evenings were given to school-work, the afternoons were a joy to everyone except Herr Anserl's pupils. Such snow as fell, fell during the nights, and the old Music master was able to get up on his regular days as usual. "Plato" came, too; but in any case, he was needed for the carol practices. But Herr Laubach and Miss Denny were told that their services, so far as teaching went, would not be required any more that term. Miss Denny came, it is true; but she taught no German or Italian. She spent her time helping with the dresses, and the School, with one accord, flung itself with might and main into the business of rehearsing.

There were carol practices, when Mr Denny became excited to the verge of losing his temper because the effect he wanted was not produced by his pupils. Miss Annersley and Miss Stewart toiled with the speaking; and, on one occasion, Evadne Lannis was discovered in tears because "Charlie" had told her that "her speaking wasn't worth a cent"—or so she reported.

"I don't believe Charlie ever used such an expression

in her life," said Jo unbelievingly. "She hates all American-isms, and won't even use quite usual words like 'stunt' or 'some.' She may have *meant* that; but I'll bet she never said it."

Miss Nalder was just as hard to please over the movements.

"Don't walk on like that as if you were having a route-march!" she was heard to cry on one occasion. Then: "Jo! *Must* you stand as if you were deformed? You can come to me after rehearsal. If you are starting curvature of the spine, I shall have to give you remedial exercises!"

Finally, Wednesday came, when the dress rehearsal was to be held, and the Tiernsee people crowded into the big hall Herr Braun, owner of the "Kron Prinz Karl," had had built for such a purpose. He himself had skated over from Buchau on the opposite side of the lake, pushing before him his wife in a chair mounted on runners. Their small granddaughter, Gretchen, was delighted to see them; but she had a part in the play, and was full of importance about it, so they did not see much of her after she had kissed them, and exclaimed aloud her joy at seeing them.

The rehearsal went off fairly well. It is true that Joey, the leading soloist, "dried up" more than once; that Mr Denny was rendered breathless with horror when the Juniors suddenly went flat in one of the prettiest of the carols; and that several people showed a tendency to stand stock-still in the most awkward attitudes at the most awkward moments. Still, as Miss Annersley said desperately at the end of it all, it is an axiom that a bad dress rehearsal generally means a good performance, so they must just trust in that and hope for the best.

Then she bade the girls put everything connected with the Pageant out of their heads, and set them to dancing once the hall had been cleared. Bed followed when they were all tired out, and they woke next day, feeling fit and fresh, and ready for anything.

*Mittagessen* was at noon, and when it was over, the girls were sent to get ready at once, for the Pageant was a long one, and was to begin at fourteen sharp. Already some parents had arrived, and were being entertained by all who could be spared from the united Staffs in the Speise-saal which, for that day, had been turned into a drawing-room.

> "And thick and fast they came at last,
> And more, and more, and more,"

quoted Joey Bettany, looking out of her window. "Robin, if you want me to fix your wings, you must hurry up. I can't play round with safety-pins when I've got floating robes all over my arms!"

The Robin, clad in her long white robes of Love, ran into the cubicle carrying with her the great wings made of buckram, with long, feather-shaped strips of white, crinkled paper gummed to them. The paper had been tinted so that to the inside of the wings it was a deep, rosy pink. They had been wired at the edge to keep them firm, and needed careful pinning to make them "set" right. Jo knelt down to wrestle with them, and pricked herself violently in the thumb. "Bother!" she ejaculated. "Now I'll bleed over everything!—Frieda, be a dear and get me the styptic from Matron, will you?"

Frieda, ready in her long, loose garments of a lady of the twelfth century, with her masses of hair hanging in thick plaits on either side of her face, caught up her floating skirts, and fled to Matron who came with the required remedy, and attended to Jo's thumb before she hastened off on a similar errand to Anne Seymour.

But at length they were all ready, and settled in the long narrow room at one side of the hall which had been christened the Green Room. The School choir which opened the Pageant were assembled on the stage behind the curtains, and there was a hum and buzz of chatter from the hall itself which told them that it was very full. Every now and then they could hear the fall of coins or the rustle of paper into the boxes set at either side of the big doors for the audience's contributions, and Marie von Eschenau voiced the thoughts of the rest when she murmured to Jo, "Oh, I do hope it's going to be a really big contribution this year, Joey! Think how much we could do with it!"

"Hush!" said Joey sharply. "There's the bell for silence!"

Then the murmuring ceased, and Mademoiselle Lepâttre's voice came from the other side of the curtains. She explained that there must be no applause, and then left the stage to take her seat in the front row with Graf von Eschenau and Mr Stevens, who, with their wives, had come especially to see this Pageant. Almost at once, the little orchestra they had collected struck up the air of the first carol—"Torches," an old Spanish carol which comes from the province of Galicia. The quaint tune was quite unknown to most people, and the young, fresh voices singing the innocent words held a charm of their own. The orchestra, though limited in numbers, was, as Frieda once remarked, very choice. Herr Anserl himself was at the piano, and Herr Helfen and Frau Linders, who taught the stringed instruments in the School, played respectively a violin and a 'cello. "Plato" added the flute, to which he was addicted, and Miss Stewart contributed a viola. The result was delightful, for all were very good, naturally, and all were heart and soul with the feeling of the Pageant.

There was a short pause after the last line of the carol, and then the curtains parted, and the Spirit of Christmas came forward. The part had been given to Simone Lecoutier, who, clad in her long gown which was looped up here and there with holly, and bearing a wreath of mistletoe and Christmas roses on her black head and a spray of fir in her hand, made a very charming Spirit. She made a short speech, welcoming all present, and then called on her faithful servants, Mistletoe, Holly, Christmas Tree, Candle, Snapdragon, Carol, Frost, and Snow, to come and tell her what they were doing for mortals.

They marched on a jolly band. Mistletoe and Holly led the way, clad in short green tunics and knickers, with clusters of their own leaves and berries about them. Christmas Tree (Thekla) wore a white underdress, the skirt of which was held out by a hoop at the hem. From waist to hem were fastened long sprays of fir, and shorter ones adorned the bodice. From the tips of the fir-sprays were hung gay glass balls, and streamers of gold and silver tinsel were twisted in and out, while her fair head was encircled by a silver band. Thekla was a tall girl, and she looked very well indeed. Candle wore a straight, up-and-down dress of stiffened white sateen, and on her yellow head was fixed a tiny electric torch, painted white, the bulb shaped like a tiny cone, and glowing golden with all its might. Snapdragon was all in weird blue and yellow, with swirling flames cut out of blue and yellow paper stiffened with wire as her headdress. With dreamy expressions, very much at variance with their usual alert ones, it was quite difficult to recognise those two imps, Cornelia and

Evadne. Carol wore a tunic of scarlet and gold, with golden notes painted on the scarlet, and she carried a scroll in one hand, on which was illuminated in glowing paints the first verse of "Stille Nacht, Heilige Nacht." Frost and Snow were all in white, Frost in a short tunic, heavily frosted, and with a gelatine crown which also gleamed with frosting; while Snow's robes were of heavy material, sweeping to the floor, and her hair was covered with a cap of cotton-wool.

But these were not all, for Peace came in, clad all in silver, and led by Goodwill who was gorgeous in crimson, and people were amazed at the difference the quaint dresses made in shy Carla and pleasant, matter-of-fact Sophie. They all saluted the Spirit, and told in blank verse of mortal doings.

Finally, there was a low, sweet strain of music, and Love drifted in—such a tender, rosy little Love, with her great wings soaring above her curly head, and a golden aureole set on her black locks. She had only a few lines to say, but she said them with such emphasis and meaning, that many people felt the truth anew, and wondered to think how little we remember Love, even on Love's own Birthday.

But they had little time for thought then, for the whole court broke into the old Czech carol "The Birds," the choir joining in from either side of the stage where they stood behind curtains.

After this, the Spirit rose from her throne, and summoned the centuries to tell their tales of Christmas doings.

> "Now that the Christmas time is very near,
> And men begin to speak of joy and mirth,
> Let us behold how, once, in days gone by,
> They hailed the sweet return of Jesu's Birth.
> Forth from the shadows, where the passing years
> Keep vigil till all time at last shall end,
> I bid you come to join our merry throng
> And to that merriment, your stories lend."

The curtains at the back of the stage parted, and a lady of the Middle Ages, clad in purple robes, with a boy and girl on either side of her, walked in, and made a sweeping reverence to the Spirit. She was followed by two jolly lads, drawing a third one perched on a Yule Log.

These came forward, and saluted the Spirit. Then they proceeded to tell of Christmas doings in their own times, of the bringing home of the Yule Log with shoutings and song; the drinking of sack and mead; of the great dish of plum porridge which graced the supper table. Finally, they gathered in a group, and, aided by the hidden choir, sang the old English carol, "Welcome Yule, thou merry man."

They took their places at the far side of the throne, and a tinkling of bells heralded the arrival of the late sixteenth-century group—parents, children and a throng of gay servitors. They sang as they came William Morris's Christmas song, "From Far Away We Come Unto You," to the setting written by Vaughan Williams. Although the audience could not understand the words, which were English, they liked its lilt and rhythm, and heads and feet went in time to the music.

This group had much to tell of the sports which took place in their time, and at once the Medievals spoke of the Boy Bishop, whose reign began on the Eve of Christmas and finished on the festival of the Holy Innocents, the greatest day of all, for on that day he celebrated the Mass, and preached from the pulpit, and all the church dignitaries must be there to listen and to watch him.

But there was a clatter of feet outside, and the children burst in from the right, clad in the gay hues of the middle of the next century. They sang, as they came, a Dutch carol known to us as "Lord Jesus hath a garden," and in their bright colours they looked like a flower-garden themselves. They spoke of dancing and masques, and were something of a contrast to the poudré group who came next, and were much more sedate. Their carol was the lovely old Austrian carol, "Ein Kindlein in der Wiegen"—or "The Baby in the Cradle."

By this time the stage was filling up, and the gay dresses and bright faces of the girls, with the Spirit high above them, surrounded by her court, while little Love nestled at the foot of the throne, was a picture not soon forgotten.

The early nineteenth century came next, the girls in long, full dresses, with pantalettes peeping beneath, while the boys wore trousers buttoned over their jackets, and what Joey called "Dog Toby" frills. They told of the Christmas Tree, brought to England from Germany by

Albert the Good, husband of the great Queen Victoria. They spoke of dear Hans Andersen's lovely story, "The Fir-Tree," and of "Struwelpeter" which was written and illustrated by Dr Heinrich Hoffmann for his little son's Christmas gift because he could find nothing gay enough for a small boy in the book line, and which has been the predecessor of special Christmas Gift Books for children. They wound up by singing the German carol, "Puer natus in Bethlehem."

Finally, the modern children came in, and they spoke of modern ways of celebrating the great Feast, stressing Santa Claus, Christmas trees, and Christmas stockings, and all the pleasures which Christmas brings to the child of to-day. The Spirit of Christmas listened very gravely, her face unusually thoughtful. They wound up by singing the well-known Holly-tree carol which is common in one version or another to nearly the whole of western Europe. Then the Spirit rose. She had something more to say.

"Christmas, ye all have told us, is the time
When men make merry—laugh, and sing, and sport.
Watch now the picture of that first sweet Day
And see how God with man did first consort.
For now, methinks, the merriment and fun
Make all forget until the time be sped
The stable, cattle, shepherds, and the straw,
The Rose of Heaven, and the Manger Bed."

Simone spoke very slowly, with deep emphasis, for she had been struck by this very thing as the groups from the various centuries had told of their doings, and she was a thoughtful girl. When she had spoken, the curtains were drawn for a moment or two, and at once there uprose the beautiful old German carol—"Ich weiss ein lieblich Engel-spiel"; or, in English, "I know a lovely angel-game." When it was finished the curtains were swept back to show the lighted stage.

A wooden manger stood in the centre, filled with straw. At one side, sitting up on his haunches, and looking at the empty manger, was Rufus, his wistful dog-face partly hidden from the audience. Behind it stood Herr Braun's pet calf, a beautiful, black-skinned creature, now half-grown, but as tame as Rufus himself. One of the Tiernsee people had sent his little grey donkey, and she was placed

153

at the foot of the manger, where she was daintily nibbling at the straw. There was nothing else; but something in the attitude of the three animals spoke of a waiting. A long sigh rose from the audience at the sight, and even the girls, who had seen it every day for a fortnight, forgot to be ready to rush forward if Taurus or Modestine—Joey had named her out of Robert Louis Stevenson's *Travels With a Donkey*—showed any sign of restiveness. All watched the scene in utter stillness.

Presently, there came three sharp knocks on the floor, and a man attired in Eastern dress came from the opposite side of the stage, and parted the curtains at the back, showing a man and a woman, also in Eastern garb.

At once the choir broke into a carol set to the old music of the Spring carol, "Tempus adest florium." This one had been written by Madge especially for the occasion, and was actually a small play.

"Dark the night and cold the wind; sleeping is the city.
   Strangers come, a bed to find."
      "Landlord, in thy pity,
   Give to us thy meanest room—we can go no longer.
   On the hills the storm-clouds loom. Hark! The wind
      blows stronger."

The choir sang only the first line and a half. The next was sung by Joey, the St Joseph of the play. Her golden voice swelled up, filling the hall with her pleading, and drawing tears to the eyes of the more emotional. Rufus stirred uneasily, but a muttered exclamation as Jo finished her song brought him back to his seat.

The landlord, Thora Helgersen, a Norwegian girl with a rich contralto voice, shook her head, and sang:

"Truth it is the night is chill, and the storm grows wilder.
   Yet we have no room so thronged we with folk and
      childer.
   Caesar's edict bade all come, each to his own city,
   For the census he would take. How may I show pity?"

Again Jo's pleading voice uprose while the hearers sat very still.

"Landlord, weary is my wife. We will ask no faring.
Such a shelter from the night as your beasts are sharing,
That we seek, a simple boon. You will not refuse us?
Surely, on this bitter night, you'll not so abuse us?"

Now the choir took up the tale for the first line of the
next verse.

"Back he stepped ungraciously; showed his straw-filled
    manger."
"Make your bed, then, with the beasts! Here, at least's
    no danger.
Here's no dread of storm and stress, and the wind's
    wild welter.
Cease this tale of your distress, you have found you
    shelter."

Thora's voice rose strong and almost harsh as befitted
the part. The travellers entered, and the landlord, having
dropped the curtains behind them, vanished, while the
choir took up the last verse.

"So, from out the bitter night and the tempest's battle,
Came Our Lady to Her rest, there amid the cattle.
Down She lay upon the straw, while the wind, once
    crying,
Ceased its fury and its roar—sang Her lullabying."

The curtains closed after that, and the orchestra played
a tender little prelude. Then the choir took up the air,
and sang in the original Latin the very old "Quem
Pastores," a German carol.

The curtains were drawn back, and there, seated by the
side of the manger and bending tenderly over it, was Marie
von Echenau, the Madonna, her lovely face intent on the
Bambino which they had borrowed from the little church
further along the lake-shore. Joey stood behind her, a
lantern held in one hand, the other resting on the neck of
Taurus who was looking gravely at the manger. Modestine
was kneeling down—the calf had refused to do it—and
Rufus lay at Marie's feet, his great head between his paws.
Groups of angels with soaring white wings were clustered
round the central figures, all with heads bent as if in
worship. The lighting fell on the manger, so that the rest
of the stage was in shadow, and the effect was startlingly

lovely. The choir sang their carol—the old Coventry carol, "Lullay, thou little tiny child." Then the curtains were closed for a moment. Suddenly the well-known music of Gounod's "Nazareth" swelled out, and a man's voice joined in, even as the curtains were swept back for the last time.

Into the stable crowded the throng of those who had kept Christmas down the ages. Quietly they came in, each kneeling in her place, and the stage was thronged. The Christmas Spirit followed with her court, little Love slipping forward to stand at the foot of the manger with one hand on Modestine's neck, her big, dark eyes on the Bambino in the crib. No words were spoken. Only that beautiful tenor voice, which no one had quite realised "Plato" possessed, rang through the room while the tiny orchestra played the soft accompaniment, and above it sounded the bells of the glockenspiel Herr Anserl had contrived to borrow from one of the Innsbruck theatres, and played by Herr Laubach with great skill. They learned afterwards that he had been glockenspielist in an amateur orchestra when he was a student.

The curtains closed for the last time while Mr Denny was singing the final verse of Gounod's "Christmas Song," and when he ended, there was a breathless silence in the hall. Accustomed as the people were to the beautiful little Christmas plays the girls gave every year, this had outstripped them all. There was not one present who did not feel the contrast between the first Christmas Day and the pleasure-filled times of later days. Madge had driven home her lesson with a sure hand. Even her own little carol told effectively.

"It is very wonderful," said big Herr Mensch later on. "These children have taught us something we are too prone to forget."

Frieda, who had doffed her medieval robes, and was now in her simple white frock, with her wonderful hair floating round her like a golden mantle, slipped her hand into his. "Madame gave the lesson, Papa," she said. "We were only—the repeaters of it."

"I wish she could have been here," said Joey coming up with the Robin, as usual, clinging to her. "Jem's an old fuss!"

"But who would have looked after the twins then?" asked Frieda.

156

"I'd forgotten the twins for once," acknowledged their aunt.

"I understand that you should wish her to see this, the finest of the plays she has given us," said Herr Mensch. "But at least we can all tell her how much we have liked it—what a good sermon she has preached us!"

Jo looked serious. "I felt—that," she said.

Little Robin lifted her face. "Now I know why we give gifts at Christmas," she said. "It is because God gave us the greatest Gift first."

"That is true, mein Liebling," said the gigantic Tirolean. "And so we shall all remember for this Christmas at least. Our dear Madame has done well for all. The Chalet School shall live and prosper."

# 'JINNY' BOOKS

## by *Patricia Leitch*

When Jinny Manders rescues Shantih, a chestnut Arab, from a cruel circus, her dreams of owning a horse of her own seem to come true. But Shantih is wild and unrideable.

This is an exciting and moving series of books about a very special relationship between a girl and a magnificent horse.

FOR LOVE OF A HORSE
A DEVIL TO RIDE
THE SUMMER RIDERS
NIGHT OF THE RED HORSE
GALLOP TO THE HILLS
HORSE IN A MILLION
THE MAGIC PONY
RIDE LIKE THE WIND
CHESTNUT GOLD
JUMP FOR THE MOON

Armada

# MILL GREEN

## School Series

### by Alison Prince

Mill Green is a big, new comprehensive — with more than its fair share of dramas and disasters! Get to know Matt, Danny, Rachel, and the rest of the First Form mob in their exciting adventures.

### Mill Green on Fire

When someone starts fires in the school and blames the caretaker, Matt is determined to catch the real culprit. But his brilliant plan to catch the firebug goes horribly wrong . . .

### Mill Green on Stage

The First Formers prepare for the Christmas pantomime — and sparks soon fly when Marcia Mudd, a ghastly new girl, gets the best part. But when Matt locks Marcia in a cupboard and she disappears from the school, there's big trouble for everyone . . .

### A Spy at Mill Green

The school is stunned when its brand-new video recorder and television camera are stolen. With all the clues pointing to an inside job, the First Formers turn detective . . .

### Hands Off Mill Green!

The First Formers can't bear the thought of Mill Green's field being sold off — especially as it was to be the site for a swimming pool. Determined to build the pool, the school starts fund-raising — but it seems the land is under a mysterious curse . . .

*More stories about Mill Green will be published in Armada.*

Armada

Here are some of the most recent titles in our exciting fiction series:

☐ Pursuit of the Deadly Diamonds *J. J. Fortune* £1.25

☐ A Leader in the Chalet School *Elinor M. Brent-Dyer* £1.50

☐ Voyage of Terror *J. H. Brennan* £1.75

☐ The Witch Tree Symbol *Carolyn Keene* £1.50

☐ The Clue in the Broken Blade *Franklin W. Dixon* £1.25

☐ The Mystery of the Purple Pirate *William Arden* £1.25

☐ Chestnut Gold *Patricia Leitch* £1.25

☐ Monsters of the Marsh *David Tant* £1.75

Armadas are available in bookshops and newsagents, but can also be ordered by post.

**HOW TO ORDER**
ARMADA BOOKS, Cash Sales Dept., GPO Box 29, Douglas, Isle of Man, British Isles. Please send purchase price plus 15p per book (maximum postal charge £3.00). Customers outside the UK also send purchase price plus 15p per book. Cheque, postal or money order — no currency.

NAME (Block letters) _____

ADDRESS _____

_____

_____